RENEE RIVA

AJ's Ireland

A Wee Little Comedy

By Renee Riva

Published by

BELLA ITALIA PUBLISHING 2015

All Rights Reserved

Edited by Lucia Garner

Cover Art by Istockphoto

ISBN:0692329048
ISBN-13:9780692329047

~FOR GINA GARNER ~FOR YOUR LOVE OF STORIES, AND YOUR
JOYFUL, ENCOURAGING HEART.

AND

FOR SOPHIA GARNER~ FOR YOUR SLIGHTLY MISCHIEVOUS, FUN
ITALIAN SPIRIT. ~

~Once upon a time there was a young Italian girl who lived in a weird family. Unfortunately, that girl was me, and those circumstances have not changed. ~

AJ Degulio

1

Happy Travels

"Oh, Danny Boy, the pipes, the pipes are calling, from glen to glen and down the mountain side..."

"AJ, could you save the Irish tunes and accent until we've landed?" Mama says from the airplane seat one row behind me.

"I have only four hours and twenty-two minutes to perfect my mother tongue," I shoot back through the narrow crack between my seat and Adriana's.

Adriana glares over at me. "Your mother's tongue, as

1

well as your father's tongue, happens to be Italian, which makes *you* Italian—unless, of course, your real parents were leprechauns, which wouldn't surprise me in the least."

"You wouldn't even be on this airplane if I hadn't won the cereal contest."

"Yeah, well, this trip had better be worth the mortification of wearing that ridiculous jumper." Adriana leans back and flips through her *Teen Beat* magazine, dismissing me.

"Yeah, you'd better promise me that I won't have to put on the dumb skirt again, or I'm not getting off this plane," my older brother, JR, says from the other side of Adriana. "Real guys just don't wear things like that."

Sigh. This family has no respect for anything non-Italian. How could staying in a real castle and learning the entire history of Ireland not be worth wearing a dumb outfit for a few minutes? It had been like pulling hen's teeth to get any of them to dress up for the contest.

My first photo was a scene from our dinner table where everyone was dressed in black and being themselves—fighting and looking miserable. Under that photo I wrote the caption **"No Ireland, No Joy."** Then we all dressed in Irish dresses and kilts that Grandma Angelina made for us and posed with happy smiles. Under that photo I wrote **"Know Ireland, Know Joy."** Two weeks later, I got a phone call from the Sugar Shamrocks people, saying that my family had won a trip to Ireland for Christmas! But does anyone in my family thank me?

I whip out my journal and write:

IRISH ROVER

Almost in Dublin, Ireland

December 1967

by AJ Degulio,

I am sitting here on a plane less than four and a half

hours from Dublin, Ireland, and cannot wait to become an

Irish Rover....

Just for sound effects while I'm writing, I start to sing very, very quietly, with only a hint of an Irish accent, *"I am a rover rolling along, a rover singing a song, I am a rover until the day I die..."*

Adriana leans over and whispers, "If you don't shut your trap right now, AJ, this *will be* the day you die."

*

Four hours, seventeen minutes later.......

Dublin, Ireland

The Blarney Bus Tours sign is waving jubilantly above the crowd in baggage claim. I grab my black suitcase and whisk it from the carousel, then head for the sign. Mama and Daddy are helping my younger twin brothers, Dino and Benji, with their luggage. Their suitcases weigh as much as they do. JR is already waiting for us by the Blarney tour group. Glamour Girl Adriana is struggling to drag her mammoth pink suitcase, along with her matching pink carry-on, across the terminal. Two handsome airport workers drop everything to assist Miss *"Aren't I the most beautiful, yet helpless, damsel in distress you've ever laid eyes on"* Adriana.

Finally, the moment I've been waiting four months for arrives. All seven of us are ushered to our luxury tour bus to set off for Christmas at the castle. The lady leading us introduces herself to Mama as Kaylee, but I missed everything else she said—I'm so excited to meet my first real Irish person in person, I just want to see if she has little elfish ears.

Out along the curb, I spot what kind of looks like the luxury bus I saw in the winner's brochure. I'm not sure the word "luxury," best describes it—looks more like the word "Blarney" was painted on over the name of the original tour bus—before it hit the guard rail, but the trip was free, so why complain?

The boys pile inside and grab seats without taking

any special notice, but not Adriana. She drops her carry-on on the top step, takes one snobby look around the bus, and says, "Leave it to you, AJ, to win us a budget vacation on the Blarney Bus."

"Would you rather be at home going to school?" I reply.

"I'd rather be in Paris, shopping." She shoves her carry-on in an overhead bin and slides across the front seat to the window.

"That wasn't an option," I counter, as I sit beside her.

Adriana looks around. "Aren't there any empty seats besides this one?" she asks. She wants me to get lost.

"Not if I want to be in the front," I tell her. "Besides, I won the trip, so I should get first pick."

She rolls her eyes.

"Welcome to Ireland!" our tour guide, Kaylee, is standing two feet in front of me, speaking into a microphone.

Maybe it's just the accent that makes me think she looks like a jolly little elf. But she *is* short and plump, and wears her hair in a silver bun on top of her head, *and* her ears do look a little elfish.

"Blarney Bus Tours is proud to escort all of you lucky winners to some of the most fascinating places in Ireland."

I thought we would be the only winners, but there are about twenty-five of us on the bus.

"We selected the three most interesting families— well, actually, two families and a group of women who are like a family. At some point along the trip we will get to enjoy a performance from each group, but it will be a surprise as to when each presentation will happen. For now, I thought it would be a fun ice breaker if you could each chose a spokesperson for your group and share how you won your ticket to Ireland."

My whole family looks at me. "You're it," JR declares.

"Yeah," Adriana adds, "you got all of us into this

mess."

Kaylee first points to a tall, attractive, woman with ravishing red hair, and asks where her group is from.

"Well, I'm Tina, and these classy gals are all Tina's Tappers. We're a tap dancing group from Washington state, and we're all forty-years-young and over." She waves her hand over her ladies like a mama hen with her chicks.

They are a pretty classy bunch, and *dressed to the nines*, as Mama would say. When my mama dresses to the nines, people often mistake her for the Italian movie star, Sophia Loren.

Tina continues, "We entered the contest with a photo of our last Christmas performance at Second Wind Retirement Home. We perform regularly in our community. We won this trip because we wanted to come to Ireland to learn your fabulous clogging method of dance, so we can bring it back to the States and bless the socks off everyone!" Tina starts to tap the toe of her shoe in the aisle like she is about to launch into a Ginger Rogers move.

I glance over at Mama, who looks thoroughly intrigued. Adriana whispers in my ear, "Let's just hope the Tappin' Grannies aren't rooming anywhere near us."

My sister is not known for compassion.

"Next, let's hear from Yancy's Yodelers!" Kaylee announces.

A loud round of yodels echo from the back of the bus. Adriana's eyes dart back to the family dressed like Hansels and Gretels. "Can it get any more painful?" she moans. "They sound more like a herd of sick mountain goats."

The father, who I'm guessing is Yancy, stands up in his yodeling knickers and states proudly, "My brood has been yodeling since the day they cut teeth; and by the end of this trip, you will all be Yancy's Yodelers."

"Over my dead body," Adriana says loudly enough to catch a raised eyebrow from Mama, who is probably thinking the same thing but has taught us not to vocalize everything we think when it comes to weird people.

"And, last but far from least, our delightful Degulio family!"

Adriana nudges me. "You're up. Don't say anything embarrassing."

I stand up and turn to face the whole busload of people. "Hi. I'm AJ, and this....this is my family." I wave my arm over them like Tina did. "There are seven of us. We don't sing or dance or nuthin' like that, but we thought it would be really fun to come here and see some castles and leprechauns and..." I look at my brothers while my mind grasps for something interesting to say, "...and we get to skip school since our school isn't out for Christmas vacation 'til next week...and...I wanted to learn to speak Irish and come home with a wee little Irish accent...and my sister didn't really want to come...until she heard that Irish boys are cu—"

Adriana's arm reaches up and yanks me back down to my seat.

"Well," Kaylee adds, "AJ sent in a very fine photograph of her family dressed in traditional Irish attire, which we will get the pleasure of seeing later this week. And here's the best surprise of all—the family with the winning performance will be featured on the next box of Sugar Shamrocks!"

The entire bus erupts into rowdy cheers and yodels ….except for six people: Mama, Daddy, Dino, Benji, JR, and Adriana.

Kaylee rambles on and on about all the places we're going to and the sights we'll be seeing. She's quite a chatty little thing. Today we'll drive through Dublin and head toward our first stop. "Ballyburrow is just outside Downpatrick. You can all get a nice meal and a good night's rest to recover from your long airplane flight."

What's there to recover from? We just sat there the

whole time.

*

"Welcome to Ballyburrow!" Kaylee's voice blares through the bus microphone, jolting me from a deep sleep. I guess I was tired after all. Twenty-five heads pop up, in a daze, like a bunch of bobblehead dolls trying to get their bearings. "We are spending our first night at the Badger's Burrow."

"Did she say burrow?" Adriana mutters. "Our room is probably underground."

Peering out the bus window, the only dwelling I see is a neat old hobbit-like hotel built into the hillside.

"Hey, where's the castle?" Dino yells.

"Ah, we'll reach the castle before Christmas—it's a bit of a drive yet, so we will enjoy a variety of interesting accommodations along the way. Tonight's stay is here at the historic Badger's Burrow."

"The word 'historic' scares me," Daddy mutters as we wait while Tina's Tappers tap dance their way down the aisle and off the bus. These women were probably all hyper kids in school who couldn't sit still. I'm glad to see there's a future for kids like that—I may be joining them one day.

We drag our luggage through the rain to the lobby, and Kaylee tells us our bags will be delivered to our rooms while we dine in the hotel restaurant, The Badger's Den.

"I certainly hope this badger theme is not going to follow us for the duration of the trip," Adriana comments as we pass by a stuffed badger. It's wearing a kilt and playing a bagpipe.

I sit between Daddy and Mama at dinner so I don't have to hear any more of Adriana's trip-spoiling commentaries. The restaurant is a cozy little den, with lots of dark wood with glowing lanterns. Rain pelts against the windows, and a warm fire crackles in an old stone fireplace. While the kitchen staff serves us bowls of hot Irish stew, Kaylee stands by the fire and says she'll give us all the rundown on the trip "itinery," whatever that is.

"Mama, what's a itinery?" I whisper.

"That's *itinerary*, Mama says. "It means she's about to give us the rundown on how this trip is going to play out."

"Oh. Okay." Then I turn to Daddy. "What did Mama mean?"

"It means what comes next."

"Ah. Why didn't Kaylee just say, 'Here's what's next?'"

"I don't know, AJ, but you're missing it by talking," Daddy remarks.

I turn my attention back to Kaylee.

"…So after our eight a.m. wake-up call…"

Adriana moans.

"…we will be back on the road to Belfast. We'll stop in Downpatrick, where we will visit the actual burial site of St. Patrick, Ireland's patron saint who died in the fifth century. We will see the memorial stone that lies where he's buried."

I raise my hand.

"Question?" Kaylee asks.

"You mean to tell me that St. Patrick has been laying there for over 1,500 years?"

"Yes, dear."

"That's a very long time."

"Brilliant deduction," Adriana whispers behind Daddy's back.

"Yes, it is a very long time." Kaylee continues, "From there we will go—"

My hand goes up again.

"Yes?"

"Well, I was going to ask—"

Adriana leans back and gives me a threatening glare. I get the message.

"Umm…never mind." *Just wondering if he was wearing green when they buried him— trying to figure out this thing about why we wear green on St. Patrick's Day.*

Kaylee continues, "From there, we will visit the Giant's Causeway…"

"Did she say *giants?*" I gasp aloud. *They* have real *giants* here?

"AJ, just eat your stew and listen," Mama whispers.

This family has no appreciation for the curiously-minded.

2

Saints and Giants

"Yodeleeeeehooooo! Yodelee-yodelee-yodeleeheeehoooo!"

We are all roused from a dead sleep by a high-pitched pack of yodelers in the hallway.

"It's time to send someone home," Adriana grumbles, from under her pillow.

JR pops his head in from the adjoining room. "This better be the only surprise presentation from the Yodel family," he says. "If this is a reoccurring wake-up alarm for the entire trip, I'm going to have to hurt someone."

JR has been watching too many shoot 'em up cowboy westerns and mob movies lately. Mama put him on TV restriction until he can stop talking like a gangster. "Crime is

17

not as glamorous as Bonnie and Clyde make it look," she told him. I think she's worried that JR might grow up to be in the Mafia. Mama already wrote to Hollywood and told them to stop making their idiotic gangster movies and airing them on prime time TV as if they were Disney films.

Adriana throws her bedspread back and swings her feet out of bed. "Bet you ten-to-one we get to wake up to the Toe-Tapping Grannies tomorrow. AJ, you're responsible for hiding all the tap shoes tonight."

Why is everything that goes wrong on this trip my fault? I wish I'd just entered that contest as an only child.

We all meet in the Badger's Den for breakfast while the hotel bellboys load our luggage back on the Blarney Bus. "Hey, wow, look at this—it's real porridge." I dump a heap of sugar on top and stir it in.

"I hate to break it to you, Goldilocks, but oatmeal is oatmeal no matter what they may call it."

Adriana has a long list of names she likes to call me;

Twit and Goldilocks are her top two, because I am the only blonde in the family, and the only one who does not look one speck Italian.

"Hey, AJ, maybe we can find your real family while we're here," she adds. "These pale people kind of look like you."

*

I can hardly wait to go see St. Patrick. All I know about him so far is that if you don't wear green on St. Patrick's Day, you get pinched, and if you wear red, you get kissed. Adriana always wears red.

Speaking of Adriana, I catch her glancing over at the Yodel family, so I look to see what she finds so interesting. I'm not surprised to find a teenage boy staring back at her. Nothing good can come from this. On the other hand, maybe Adriana can convince Yodel Boy not to wake us up again with his horrible call of the wild. This should at least make the rest of the trip more bearable and keep Adriana from complaining so much. I bet she's already changed her mind about wanting to send the Yodel family home. I really don't like that my sister is boy crazy, but having someone around who can keep her from whining for the rest of the trip may not be such a bad thing. Even if he is dressed up in a Hansel costume.

Clearly, Kaylee has picked this morning for the Yodel family to do their thing. I think my family was hoping that their yodeling wake-up call was the extent of their surprise performance, but, guess not. Kaylee ushers them to the front of the room to "give us their best."

Their family line-up includes: Papa Yancy, Mama, two older boys, and two little kids; one girl and one boy. I didn't catch their names because I was too busy thinking up names I thought they should have; for starters: Heidi for Mama, and Gretal for the little girl.

Papa Yancy lauches the whole thing off with a big Yodelee-yodelee-yodelee-hee-hoo… then they go down the line joining in. I find the whole thing pretty fascinating but being in such a small room, their yodels bounce and echo all over. By the time they are done, my ears are ringing.

"Well, that was awkward," Dino says to Benji.

My parents have taught us to always be cordial to awkward people, so we all have cordial smiles on our faces, especially Adriana, who has somehow managed to look beyond the cry of the "sick mountain goats" to the handsome face behind the knickers and suspenders.

Climbing back on the bus, I notice that Adriana has grabbed a seat for us directly in front of Yodel Boy and his little brother. Maybe it's time I strike out and meet some new friends. I bet any one of those tapper ladies is nicer than my sister. I look around for one of them, but everyone already has a seat buddy. For now, I'm stuck.

As soon as I sit down, Adriana stands up. "The little gentleman in the seat behind us is trading with me." My sister sweeps past me.

"Whoa….what?"

The next thing I know, a kid about twelve comes scooting into Adriana's seat. "Uh, hi," he says. He looks like he feels as embarrassed about this as I do. "Sorry about this. My big brother made me sit here so he can talk to your sister."

Imagine my surprise. "The story of my life," I say.

"Yeah, mine too," he mutters.

I realize this isn't his fault any more than it's mine— we are just two victims of deranged older siblings. "I'm AJ."

"I'm Noah."

"As in the ark?"

"Exactly. What does AJ stand for?"

"Antoinette Jezzabella."

"Really?"

"No. It's really Angelina Juliana. I just thought my real

name might not sound so bad if I used a worse name first."

He laughs. "That's funny. It does sound a little better when you put it like that."

"You can call me AJ."

"Okay. You can call me No."

This boy is actually more interesting than my sister. "So where'd you learn to yell—er, yodel—like that?"

"My grandfather is from Switzerland. We're Swiss, so we have to yodel. Family tradition and all that." Noah rolls his eyes.

"Oh, believe me, I know all about family traditions. We're Italian. How do you think I got stuck with my name?"

"Grandparents?"

"Exactly. Both grandmothers."

"Well, thank goodness I wasn't the oldest son. My big brother got stuck with my great-grandfather's name, Hans.

Do you have a lot of relatives?"

"Do we ever! We have some of the weird…uh, most *interesting* relatives you could ever meet. Some of them live in Italy and some in America. The ones in America are…let's just say, *really* interesting."

"Really?" Noah's eyes light up. "Can you give me an example?"

"Well, okay. This family, the Sophronios, they have two kids: Cousin Nicky and Cousin Stacy. Stacy is fifteen, like my sister, and just like my sister, she will do *anything* to get attention. It's usually my mama who steals the show wherever we go. But my mama has a sister—Aunt Genevieve—who is Stacy's mama. She's married to a big Greek, my Uncle Nick.

"Anyway, we all went to a family wedding last summer. One of our other cousins got married. Just before the bride came down the aisle, Cousin Stacy came waltzing into the church wearing this dress that looked like it was straight off the set of *Gone With the Wind*; I mean billows of purple ruffles with a full-blown hoopskirt underneath, making her stick out three feet in every direction. And she wasn't even a bridesmaid! She had her hair done up in big ol' curls and ribbons. On top of that, this dress did nothing for her 'big boned' figure; my daddy said she looked like one of those Southern dolls with the crocheted dresses that grandmothers put around toilet paper rolls on the back of toilets."

"My grandma has one of those toilet paper roll dolls," Noah exclaimed.

"Mine, too. Anyway, everyone was so floored by Cousin Stacy, no one even noticed the bridesmaids coming in behind her, not to mention the bride!"

"No kiddin'?" Noah says.

"No joke. My mama was shocked that Aunt Genevieve would let her daughter upstage the bride like that, but then, if you knew my relatives, you'd understand."

The story of my troublesome cousins is cut short

when Kaylee comes on the speaker to announce that we are passing Drogheda, the scene of the Battle of the Boyne in 1690.

"Cool," Noah remarks. His attention is instantly drawn out the bus window to where the battle took place. Wars are hard to compete with when you're talking to a boy.

It makes me too sad to think of these beautiful green fields with brave soldiers and gallant horses getting blown up all over the place. My mind just can't go there. When I see or hear about anything suffering, I feel like it's me in their place, and I just go crazy. I'm safer just thinking about St. Patrick and the giant.

After driving through the Mourne Mountains, we finally arrive at Downpatrick and pull up to a huge old cathedral on a hillside.

I can see how this place has lasted so long. It's made of rock-solid gray stone. And there are big grave stones sticking up out of the ground all over, too. I'm not used to seeing headstones and graves right in the front yard of a church, but there they are, just plain as day, surrounding the whole church.

We're directed toward St. Patrick's grave. Kaylee says we're free to wander both outside and inside the cathedral. When I see the big memorial stone with the name *Patric* all worn down, I suddenly really get it. I kind of thought saints were more like angels. But there is a real person lying under that stone—well, his body is; probably, his soul is in heaven, which is a good thing because 1,500 years is a long time to lie in the same place. I'm tempted to let the priest here know that they spelled Patrick's name wrong on his memorial stone, but if they haven't noticed the missing *k* for this long, why bother them with it now?

Kaylee tells us that Patrick was a brave boy who was kidnapped from his family home in Britain and forced into slavery for six years in Ireland. After he escaped, he heard the cry of the Irish in a dream and went back to Ireland to help the people find God.

It makes me wonder why St. Patrick's Day in America is only about leprechauns, beer, wearing green, and pinching people. The real story is much more interesting.

Adriana and Yodel Boy, who I guess is the one named Hans, are looking at each other instead of taking in these historical wonders. I get queasy watching them, so I escape inside the church. There are huge gold pipes from an old pipe organ that run all the way up the wall, and bright stained glass windows on the side walls of the church.

My favorite window is the one of Saint Brigid. Kaylee says that Brigid was a slave, like her mama. Her father was her mama's master. When she was a kid, she heard St. Patrick preach and was inspired to follow God. She loved everyone and couldn't bear to see anyone who was hungry or cold, so she gave away a lot of her father's food and clothing to help the poor. When her father caught her and asked why, she said, *"Christ dwells in every creature"*. Her angry father tried to sell her to the king, but when the king saw her handing a silver sword to a poor family, he said

Brigid was more noble than any of them, and he set her free. "She is remembered for her high spirits and tender heart," Kaylee concludes.

I sure hope someone remembers my high spirits that way one day. I have a ways to go yet, but I have always wanted to be a good little soul.

*

After we all get a good look around, it's back on the bus to the Giant's Causeway. I have a feeling this is where my imagination is going to go wild. I'm intrigued at the mention of giants, elves, leprechauns, and trolls. I don't hear these words much back home. Are they myths, legends, fables, or facts?

Since the teenage lovebirds are already sitting next to each other, Noah and I settle into the same arrangement as before. I take the seat by the window, and Noah slides in next to me, a little less reluctant this time.

"Hey, AJ," he says, "Can you tell me another story about your relatives? It makes the trip go faster."

"Well," I think for a moment. "Do you want to hear about the time we visited the cousins for the Fourth of July and played F-Troop on horseback, until Cousin Nicky ruined it for everyone?"

"Yeah."

"Okay." I scoot around in my seat and get as comfortable as I can for this saga. "Normally, we get really excited about the Fourth of July, but this year we knew it was ruined as soon as my mama told us we were going to our Greek cousins' dude ranch."

I remembered the moment. "We were eating Velveeta grilled cheese sandwiches, and the entire dinner table got instantly silent. Even though the Degulios are never silent." Noah laughs at this.

"We stopped mid-bite into our sandwiches—melted Velveeta cheese strands sliding down our faces. Even though Mama tried to say this in her 'won't this be fun?' voice, it just didn't fly. Daddy said he would prefer to stay home and blow himself up with a bundle of firecrackers."

"But a *dude ranch?* I have *always* wanted to go to a dude ranch!" Noah objected.

"It's not so much the ranch, as the relatives who *run* the ranch. They always try to make Daddy feel like a loser for being a park ranger instead of a multi-millionaire like Uncle Nick. When we spent Memorial Day there, Daddy had to put up with Uncle Nick's wisecracks all night. On top of that, when they took us all out for a trail ride, Uncle Nick thought it would be funny to give Daddy the mule named Buck, who they named for obvious reasons. My poor daddy had a very rough ride. Uncle Nick and Cousin Nicky laughed their fool heads off every time Buck bucked. Daddy couldn't walk right for a week. He swore he would never spend another weekend on the Double N Ranch; named after the two Nicks, but Daddy calls it the 'Double Nuts Ranch'—when Mama's not around."

"So did he go back on the Fourth of July?" Noah asks.

"Yes, but only because Mama told him Uncle Nick would be too busy getting ready for his rodeo to worry about getting Daddy back in the saddle."

"So what happened?" Noah leans closer. I usually don't get this much interest in my stories, so I decide to give it to Noah blow-by-blow. My teacher says that makes for good storytelling.

"Well, we pulled up in our station wagon and were greeted with official Greek hospitality; Uncle Nick strutted across the driveway in his cowboy boots and ten-gallon cowboy hat. Scrawny little Nicky Jr. came strutting up right behind him with his alligator boots and a pair of spurs on. He had what looked like a two-gallon cowboy hat, and it was on backwards and looked ridiculous. They both had on plaid cowboy shirts that looked like they came straight from the local Wigwam store and hadn't been broken into yet.

"See, my uncle has a very successful import business that his Greek relatives help manage, so he takes on big hobbies in his spare time. This dude ranch is his latest fling, as my daddy calls it. Before that it was horse racing, but they never won a single race so they traded their race horses in for rodeo horses. It will be interesting to see how long this rodeo thing *flings*.

"Anyway, Big Nick yelled, 'Howdy y'all!' which sounded very unnatural coming from the mouth of a big Greek. Last year, they all came home from a two-week vacation in England with British accents." *Although I secretly hope it happens to me here in Ireland.* "Then Cousin Nicky laid a 'Howdy, folks,' on us, trying to sound all cowboy-gruff. I asked where Cousin Stacy was, hoping to get away from Nicky before he pulled his rope out.

"The first time we were at the ranch, Nicky spent the whole time trying to lasso me and hog tie me, all because I turned their caged bunnies free to escape their impending doom. I was just admiring how soft and sweet their litter of eight baby bunnies was, when Nicky spouted off about how his mama was going to cook them all up in a bunny-pot-pie for Easter. I took one look at those innocent little faces looking at me like they wanted to be free so bad they were about to scream. Well, that was all it took for me to set the captives free, and off they all hopped into the woods to freedom.

"So anyway, Nicky said Stacy was 'up yonder in the mess hall.' What he calls a *mess hall* is really a huge cedar and stone *lodge* that's more of a mansion.

"Adriana followed me up to the lodge, but my brothers got corralled by the 'double Nicks' to go down to the barn to see the new rodeo horse they just bought for Stacy.

"When we got to the kitchen, Stacy was showing off her new outfit. She looked like *Strawberry Shortcake Goes to the Rodeo.* Let's just say, I had never seen pink fringed chaps or pink crocodile riding boots until right that very minute. I just hoped the new rodeo horse didn't have a problem with the color pink."

"So, when did you get to ride the horses?" Noah asked.

"Well, it was right after dinner when all the fun really started. Since the cousins and Uncle Nick were busy with the rodeo horses, they told us we could ride their pleasure horses 'til they finished. We would all gather after dark to blow off fireworks. Personally, I thought it was crazy to make all that noise around the horses, but they said their horses were used it."

"What were the names of the horses?" Noah asked.

I'm getting the feeling that Noah is way more into the horses than he is my cousins. "I got to ride Sundance, the Palomino. JR got Blue, who was really white, and the twins got the ponies: Donner and Prancer, who looked nothing like reindeer. So while my parents and Adriana were stuck getting a personal tour of Aunt Genevieve's walk in closet, the four of us hit the trails.

"We were riding along the back fence that nudges up to their neighbor's property, when JR got beaned in the head by a flying walnut. It came from over the neighbor's fence. That's when we saw three kids on their horses on the other side of the fence.

"'Hey, what'd you do that for?' JR yelled at 'em.

"'Oh, sorry, we thought you were the weird kid that lives there,' the oldest guy yelled back. 'He's always shootin' his B-B gun at us.'

"'That's my cousin!' JR yelled back at him. 'He's not with us, and we don't have any BB-guns.'

"They rode out from behind the trees to see us. We all introduced ourselves, and JR said, 'Hey, you guys want to play F-Troop with us?' That's our favorite Calgary and Indian TV show.

"They were all for it. They had bows and arrows with rubber tips, so they were the Indians. We gathered pinecones for grenades and were the Calgary. We all agreed not to throw walnuts—those hurt.

"So me and my brothers gathered a whole pile of pinecones while the neighbors ran to get their weapons. As soon as that first arrow flew, we started hurling our grenades over the fence. After all the arrows were on our side of the fence, we switched. They gave us their bows to shoot the arrows back at them, and we became the Indians. They gathered all our pinecones and became the Calgary."

Noah looks fascinated. "That sounds so fun."

"It was, until Nicky rode up with his BB-gun, fired a shot over the fence, and ruined the whole game. We were just about to ride back and shoot off the fireworks when Nicky started tossing lit firecrackers over the fence at the neighbor kids. We were so mad at him and were all yelling, 'Stop it, Nicky!' But he didn't stop—until my daddy showed up and pulled him off his horse by the scruff of his neck. That was enough reason for Daddy to call it an early night, and loaded our family back into the station wagon. Uncle Nick tried to convince him to stay, and said, 'Hey, lighten up a little, Sonny. Kids will be kids.'

"Daddy said, 'Not if *lighten up* means letting a kid *light up* an entire forest.'

"It's hard to convince a park ranger that tossing a lit firecracker into a dry forest is merely a kid being a kid. Not in our family anyway."

"Wow. I wish we had stories like that," Noah replied. "The only thing that comes close was when a neighbor shattered our window with a rock for yodeling too loud and driving his family nuts."

I can kind of understand that.

3

Oh Danny Boy

Our bus is winding all over these squirrely country roads on a downhill slope toward the sea. When we finally reach the coastline, we take a long, steep road all the way down to sea level. Right before our eyes are hundreds of stepping stones that jut up out of the shoreline and look like, well, stepping stones for giants. They are all different heights, from ground level to about 40 feet high. Legend says they really *were* stepping stones for the giant who built the causeway; a path above the water.

Kaylee starts telling the story the second we step off the bus.

"The giant was fifty-four feet tall, and he was called Finn. Finn lived happily on the Antrim coast with his wife

Oonagh until he discovered he had a rival in Scotland, named Benandonner. Benandonner often taunted Finn from afar. On one occasion, Finn scooped up a clod of earth and hurled it across the sea, but missed. The dirt landed in the middle of the Irish Sea, making the Isle of Man, and the depression formed from scooping up the earth filled up with water and became Lough Neagh."

I am picturing all of this while we are actually stepping on these very stones. "Finn finally challenged Benandonner to a proper fight and decided to build a causeway of enormous stepping stones across the sea to Scotland, so he could walk across without getting his feet wet. But as he approached and caught sight of the great size of Benandonner, Finn became afraid and fled back home, with Benandonner hot on his trail. Finn lost one of his great boots, and today it can be seen where it fell to the ground on the foreshore in Port Noffer.

"When Finn got home, he asked Oonagh to help him hide. Clever Oonagh dressed Finn as a baby and pushed him into a huge cradle. When Benandonner saw the size of the sleeping 'child,' he assumed the father—the man he was supposed to fight—must be gigantic. Benandonner ran home in terror, ripping up the causeway behind him, in case he was followed. Both giants kept to themselves after that. But this is the reason that the Giant's Causeway exists in Ireland."

Noah and I look at each other, amazed. "Is that a true story?" I ask him, loud enough that my sister hears me and shakes her head in disgust. But how am I supposed to know that really big people didn't live here a long time ago? Dinosaurs are huge, and they were real.

Noah and I climb all over the causeway, pretending to be Finn and Benandonner, until the cold wind makes my hands and feet so numb that I can't feel them anymore. JR comes over and hangs out with Noah while I hobble back to the bus to warm up. I watch from the window as Tina's Tappers actually tap dance on the causeway all the way back to the bus.

"Just trying to keep our toes warm," Tina says, as she taps her way up the bus stairs. Once everyone returns to the bus, we head up the hill to a café where they bring us hot chocolate and Malteser Bars, which are crunchy chocolate cookies with malt balls inside, to help us thaw out. I wish they had food like this in America. Maybe Mama can bribe them for the recipe.

*

After a lo-o-o-ng bus ride along the coast, we finally arrive in the town of Sligo. Our hotel is very old and pretty. There are black and white checkerboard floors in the lobby and little velvet couches. Pictures of the olden days hang on all the walls, and I get carried away looking at them, then realize everyone else has gone upstairs to their rooms to change out of their damp, salty beach clothes.

Today's *itinerary* said everyone is on their own tonight to explore the town. Our family gets to go to a real pub for dinner. They even let kids inside pubs here as long as we don't stay past dinner. When I asked Daddy why, he said, "That's when all the beer and cigarettes come out." Who would want to stay for that anyway?

I find my little brothers running up and down the hall, and follow them back to our room. Daddy tells me to go wash up so we can go get some pub grub. Kaylee tags along behind us when we leave. It's raining, but people here walk everywhere no matter what.

"Sligo is translated as 'abounding in shells,'" Kaylee informs us. "Tomorrow we will see the Famine Memorial on the Quays, but for now, go enjoy a good Irish feast!"

Something about going from feast to famine overnight sounds all wrong. At least it's probably better this way; I might feel too guilty to eat if it were the other way around.

Our family walks about four blocks to a pub called Willy O' Riley's. I start to sing *Sweet Molly Malone*, about a little dead girl who "still wheels her wheelbarrow down streets broad and narrow, singing, cockles and mussels, alive, alive-O."

Adriana leans over and threatens to put me in the Sugar Shamrock's raffle as the door prize, if I don't stop singing.

"I can't help singing Irish songs with an Irish accent when I'm in Ireland."

"Well, get over it."

The bright lights and crackling fire draw me right through the door to a table next to the fireplace. It's very cozy inside, like being in someone's living room with people eating and drinking and chatting away.

There are only a few dinner options to choose from— not like back home where you have fifty choices. It's more like a chalkboard with "take it or leave it." Tonight it's Irish stew with potatoes, or corned beef and cabbage. Benji and Dino ask for hamburgers. The waitress says she'll see what she can do. I try to order spaghetti, but it doesn't work. She doesn't even say she'll try. All I get is an elbow in the ribs from Adriana. I go with the stew.

Partway through the meal, I get up to use the restroom. I have to pass by the bar to find it. There are a bunch of men there, all talking in strong accents, and it gives me an idea.

On my way back to my table, I walk up to a nice-looking Irishman. "Excuse me, sir, but can I ask you something?"

"Aye," he says.

"Do you know the words to *Danny Boy?*"

A big grin crosses his face. "Do I know the words to *Danny Boy?*" All the men start to laugh like that's funny to them. "Lassie, everyone in Ireland knows the words to *Danny Boy,*" he says.

"Well, do you think you could all come over and sing it to my family at that table by the fire? My daddy will probably buy you some beer."

They look at each other and laugh again. "We'd be happy to!" They all take the last few gulps from their beer mugs, then follow me to our table. I sit down like nothing unusual is about to happen, while they all make a horseshoe around our table and sing away—every verse, every word—of their beautiful Irish ballad in their beautiful accents.

I am in heaven. Mama, Daddy and JR are slowly coming on board. The twins just keep eating their Irish hamburgers. And Adriana's face looks shocked and red the whole time, like she really wants to hit me.

By the last verse, everyone in the entire pub is singing *Danny Boy*. At the end, I give them a standing ovation and yell, *"Bravo!"* while moving a good arms-length away from Adriana—just in case.

While I'm walking the men back to the bar, one of them asks me if I know what the song *Danny Boy* is about.

"A love song about a girl saying good bye to her boyfriend?" I guess.

"That's what many people think, but it's actually a song from a father to his son during the great famine. You see, Lass, when the people in Ireland were starving, many families had to split up to survive. This father is telling his son that the pipes are calling him to the harbor when the ship comes to take him away to a new land so he can survive. The father is old and is saying goodbye because he is going to stay and take his fate. He tells the lad, 'But come ye back when summer's in the meadow,' and if he has died, he wants his son to kneel on his grave and say a prayer for him, then he will rest in peace until they meet again."

That is the saddest song I have ever heard.

*

We are standing on the Quay, looking at the Great Potato Famine Memorial. It's very hard for me to see things like this. There are life-sized statues of Irish people from the middle of the 1800s, when everyone in Ireland was starving and a million people died. A potato blight killed all their crops, so they had nothing to eat. A million more emigrated to other countries to survive.

After seeing skinny statues of kids my size, and sad mamas carrying hungry babies, I have to go stare out to sea and think about the ones who got onto ships that took them to a new land with food. I stare and stare, picturing them crossing the waters day after day, then reaching land where people bring them some nice warm soup, and that helps me stop crying.

*

After lunch, we get right back on the bus and make our way south to the Cliffs of Moher. Kaylee promises that this is part of the journey to get to our castle, and once we get there, we'll get to sleep in the same bed for the rest of the trip. But we still have a ways to go.

Stepping off the bus, I am amazed at how high the Cliffs of Moher really are. Kaylee says they are 668 feet high. And they just go on and on and on along the coastline forever. It's like standing at the top of the Grand Canyon with the ocean down below. I'm glad to see a rock fence along the edge, because when you look 668 feet down it can make you very dizzy. And when you look out, you can see all the way to Scotland and probably to America, too, on a clear day, but I haven't seen a clear day yet.

JR takes pictures of the twins pretending to climb over the ledge. I take a picture of Mama nearly having a heart attack. I ask the guide how many people have fallen off the cliff into the sea, and when he tells me, I decide to go visit the gift shop and listen to some calming Irish music. I'm kind of accident prone.

The gift shop has headphones to listen to their music, so I just curl up in a big, soft chair and listen away. The next thing I know, JR is shaking me awake and telling me that everyone's been looking all over for me, and the bus has been waiting to leave for almost an hour. I didn't tell anyone when I left the cliff, so of course, Mama and Daddy are frantic, thinking I fell off somewhere along the way.

It's rather embarrassing to walk down the aisle of a bus when everyone has been either looking for you or waiting for you. All the front seats are taken, so I have to walk the path of humility all the way to the back of the bus, with Mama storming down the aisle behind me, yelling *'Angelina Juliana Degulio!'* with that motherly 'I'm relieved-you're-alive,' but 'boy-are-you-in-trouble,' tone in her voice.

I quickly slip in next to Noah and pull out my journal to hide my face in the pages while I write:

No one will remember this 5 years from now.

4

Are We There Yet?

Irish Rover ; Back on the Bus! Ennis to Dingle

Last Night we stayed in a cute little cottage-like hotel in Ennis. Slept like a *mummy* after spending the past few days in the *Land of Giants,* and trolls. Today we have been on the bus since dawn. They did let us out at another troll village called Adare. I call them troll villages 'cause they have cute little thatched roof cottages lining the town. They look like the kind of thing a troll would live in. We didn't stay long. It was a short town.

When we were all back on the bus and ready to leave, we realized two people were still missing: Adriana and Hans.

Someone said they saw them at the other end of town, so Rory just fired up the bus and drove down Main Street looking for them. There they were, sitting on a park bench staring into each other's eyes, clueless that the entire Blarney Bus was watching them. Just as Hans was moving in to try and lock lips with my sister, Daddy stormed off the bus and yelled, "Adriana, you have three seconds to get your tail back on this bus!"

When Adriana looked over and saw the entire busload of people staring at her, she looked horrified. It was great. She got me off the hook for being late last time—at least I was only asleep instead of gawking into the eyes of some Yodeler about to plant his slobbery lips all over me.

Adriana leans over. "What are you writing about now? Little elves and fairies?"

"Yeah, a yodeling elf named Hans who kisses a wicked fairy named Adriana. He turns into a toad."

She glares at me. "That book is fire starter if you say one word about me."

Too late. I close my journal. We are now on a thirty-two mile roller coaster ride along the Dingle Peninsula. I wish it were a real roller coaster, but all these twists and turns on a bus still make me a little queasy. Every time I feel carsick, I just stare out the window at the ocean, and it keeps me from making them stop the bus so I can throw up.

I like all the little stone houses and rock walls that everyone has for fences here. There are lots of sheep and some very interesting herds of Oreo-cookie cows. They have black heads and rear ends, with a big white stripe around their middle—just like an Oreo cookie. But my favorite thing of all are the Gypsy Vanner horses. They're hefty black and white draft horses with furry hooves. I have been begging Daddy to ship one home for me for Christmas, but he just laughs. He says our backyard isn't big enough.

"Can we stop and pet the Gypsy horses, Kaylee?" I ask as our bus whizzes past a huge hillside of them.

"Not just now, but I believe there is a small horse at the castle in Killarney."

She just made my trip.

Benji pipes up from the back, "Hey, when are we getting to the castle, anyway?"

"Yeah, why aren't we there yet?" Dino chimes in.

"Soon," Kaylee replies. "Killarney will be our next stop."

"Yay!" The boys yell. "It's about time we get off this dumb bus!"

Mama turns around and gives them *the look.* They go back to shooting imaginary Vikings out the bus windows.

I have a burning question I'm dying to ask Kaylee, but will just write it down for now and wait until Adriana is not around to make fun of me.

Irish Rover

My burning question is: If we wash a sweater made out of sheep's wool and put it in the dryer, it shrinks to the size of a doll sweater. So if it rains on the sheep all the time, and they dry in the warm sun, why don't they shrink?

About an hour after my stomach says, "Enough is enough on this darn bus!" the Blarney Bus turns up a tree-lined drive to a *very* old stone castle. "Here we are!" Kaylee announces. " Welcome to Blarney Beag!"

The bus goes quiet.

"That's a castle?" Adriana asks, in her *I don't believe*

it tone.

"Blarney Beag means Little Blarney. It was built as a small replica of the real Blarney castle."

"What's a *replica?*" I ask.

"In this case it means a small copy-cat castle of the real Blarney Castle—the one that has the Blarney Stone."

"Hey look!" Dino yells. "There's a moat around it!"

"Cool!" Benji shouts his approval.

It's not that it's a bad little castle. It's just really small for a castle—like a baby castle. Probably about the size of our two story JC Penny store back home. It's not fancy smansy, but it is kind of cute. It has ridges around the top like a real castle and a round tower like a Rupunzle tower. It's just not like a Cinderella castle. And the moat is like a donut of water that surrounds it. There's even a little rowboat you can row around the moat in.

"The best part of it being small," Kaylee says, "is that

we get the whole castle to ourselves. Our group will be the only guests staying here."

"We're probably the only people they could get to book it," Adriana mumbles. "Leave it to Sugar Shamrock's bargain budget tour."

You could put Adriana in a gondola in Venice and she'd complain that there's only one oar. The ingrate. I, on the other hand am always looking for the silver lining, and my eyes just found it. Behind the rock wall surrounding the castle, is a fuzzy little donkey straining to look over the wall to greet us. He can barely get his muzzle over the top. "Hey, who's the donkey?" I ask.

"That is little Paddy," Kaylee says. "He's the castle's mascot. You're welcome to pet him and feed him carrots any time."

I am outta here.

I am off the bus as soon as it stops moving and climb the rock wall to Paddy's pen in no time flat. In minutes, I have little Paddy's head resting on my lap while I sit on top of the stone wall and scruff his cute fuzzy ears and face. I have no idea what a mascot is, but to me, Paddy is *The Gallant Little Steed of Baby Blarney Castle.*

It feels so good to be off that bus. I was getting worried that my rear end might become the permanent shape of a bus seat. I watch my brothers, along with Noah, race all over the castle grounds, turning sticks into swords and throwing rock grenades into the moat. This is a kid's paradise. We have finally found what we came to Ireland for: castles and moats, green grass, fresh salty air, and a fuzzy little donkey named Paddy. We are all in our happy place…except, of course, Adriana, who is still ranting away.

"This is *not* a castle! This is a *dump*. An old, crumbling, *rock dump*…wha-wha-wha-blah-blah-blah…."

Who rang her chimes? Geez!

Fortunately, Adriana wanders out of earshot with her proclamations of doom and gloom. You almost have to feel sorry for someone who can't see the silver lining anywhere. It's like she has this personal little rain cloud that follows her everywhere she goes and rains on everything she sees. *Drip...drip...drip.* I hope that isn't something that happens to all teenagers, or I don't ever want to be one.

Mama and Daddy stroll by to say hello and meet Paddy. They know where to find me anytime I'm missing— just look for the animals. "Hey, kiddo," Mama says. "You should go check out our castle suite. We have an entire wing to ourselves."

"Really? Do I have my own room?" *Please, please, please—no more Adriana; spoiler of dreams.*

"Well, it's not quite that big, but we have a nice sitting room with a fireplace and three bedrooms off that. Daddy and I have the *King and Queen's Suite*, the boys have the *Knights' Quarters, and* you and Adriana have the *Princess Parlor.* It's at the top of the winding staircase on the right."

"Wow. I'll check it out before dinner. I'll probably need a shower if I don't want to smell like a donkey."

"Good point," Daddy says.

They stroll off holding hands. I'm glad my Mama and Daddy still like each other. It's nice to see grownups who still hold hands after having a bunch of wild kids who drive them crazy. Speaking of crazy, my brothers are all lying along the moat, presumably dead, with their stick swords stuck between their arms and their sides. Mortal wounds. The battle is over. It's time for someone to play "Taps."

The dinner gong brings them all instantly back to life. They jump up and run inside. Guess I'd better go, too, if I want to catch a quick shower first. Kaylee said the gong would be a 30 minute warning. I hope they have hot water here.

The lobby of Blarney Beag has huge wood beams, a big stone fireplace, and fancy high-back chairs that look like thrones sitting in front of it. A grand old staircase curves up to the next floor, leading to our suite. We get the whole east wing. Even the door to our suite is a real castle door—tall and heavy with a brass knocker. I don't even bother to try the knob, 'cause I just want to use the knocker. I bang the brass ring nice and loud until JR opens the door. "Oh, sorry, no solicitors." He slams the door in my face.

I pound the ring even louder. I can hear Mama yelling through this thick wooden door. "JR, let your sister in this instant before I call the guards to take you to the dungeon!"

The door slowly opens.

Our sitting room is royal red and has a fireplace and fancy chairs like the ones in the lobby. Our *Princess Parlor* is fancy-smancy, with two canopy beds. I have *always* wanted to sleep in one of these beds!

Adriana has stopped complaining, which is her way of saying she likes something. I just remind her, "You can't judge a castle by its cover."

"That's brilliant," she replies in a dull voice, then dips her fingers back in her jar of Dippity-do and rolls a giant curler on top of her head.

After jumping up and down on my fancy bed for a few minutes, I waltz into our private bathroom with the hand-carved Gaelic mirror and old fashioned bathtub. I dump in the entire bottle of bubble bath and blast the water, pretending I'm a real princess. It feels so good to soak my bus-weary bum in this tub of bubbles. I never want to sit on a bus that long ever again.

I soak long enough to sing three rounds of *Sweet Molly Malone* in full Irish accent, and belt out the last and final verse as loud as I can:

> *"She died of a fever,*
> *And no one could save her,*
> *And that was the end of sweet Molly Malone.*
> *But her ghost wheels her barrow,*
> *Through streets broad and narrow,*
> *Crying, 'Cockles and mussels, alive, alive, O!'"*

"Hey, AJ!" Adriana yells. "You're going to be *wheeling your barrow through streets broad and narrow* in a bath towel if you don't cut the cockles and mussels, right now!"

I decide it's a good time to climb out. Reaching for the fluffy white towels, I crack open the bathroom door to let all the steam out. I can't see myself in the mirror anymore. "Oh, servant girl!" I call to Adriana, through the crack in the door, "Can you bring me my robe and some crackers?"

The crack in the door suddenly slams shut. I guess my servant girl is busy with other chores right now. "Just bring them when you're done mopping the floors, then," I yell back.

On the way to the *Royal Dining Room*, I find the boys running up and down the halls, searching for secret doors and passageways that will lead to underground tunnels and hidden jewels. Mama and Daddy are still holding hands, smiling that their brood is finally happy. And Adriana is checking her hair in all the hallway mirrors, making sure her Dippity-do hairdo is still sky-high. She is already nearly six feet tall, and the giant, poofy rat's nest on top of her head adds another half foot. Adriana just *has to* stand out in a crowd. The bigger the crowd—the higher the hair.

I'm wearing my denim overalls, but in my imagination,

I am three inches taller than Adriana, and am in a winter-white faux rabbit fur gown with matching booties and a crystal tiara.

The *Royal Dining Room* is just the way I hoped it would look—like the kind of place King Arthur would sit with all of his knights and gnaw on a drumstick. We are seated at a long, long table that's big enough for all three of our groups. I love these tables, and I love that we are free to sit anywhere we want so we can meet new people. I sit with Noah on one side and Netti, one of Tina's Tappers, on the other side.

Netti is just a cute, tiny lady who reminds me of my Grandma Angelina. She's very smiley and friendly, so I decide to tell her about meeting Paddy the donkey. She seems so interested that I ask if she would like to hear the story I made up about Paddy while I was sitting on that rock wall.

"Why, yes, dear, I would love to hear it."

So I tell her: "Once there was a little Irish donkey, and a little girl who loved him dearly. But the little girl had a mean step sister who wanted to become a princess. One day, she took the little donkey away from the little girl to ride it to the ball to meet the prince. The step sister had big poufy hair, and when she climbed on the little donkey's back, it scared the dickens out of him and he ran away with the step sister screaming her head off. The little girl who loved the donkey missed him terribly. One day, when the sad little girl was sitting by the rock wall, the gallant little donkey returned. They were both so happy again. Sadly, the mean step sister fell off somewhere in the Enchanted Forest and was never seen again. And we all lived happily ever after."

*

While we're all stuffing ourselves silly on pot roast and potatoes, Netti asks me if I would like to hear a little story of hers.

I nod enthusiastically, with my cheeks too full to

speak.

"Well, when I was a young girl, right about your age, I had an older sister. She wasn't very kind to me. She thought of me as a little tag-a-long and a bit of a nuisance. She often had to look after me because we were very poor, without a papa, and our mama had to work. My sister saw me as a burden and I think she kind of resented me for that. But one day, our mama got very ill, and before we knew it, our mama was gone too. And do you know what happened to my sister and I?"

"No….what?" I whispered.

"Well, the two of us looked at each other and realized we were the only family we had left. And you know, we have been best friends ever since." Netti gave me a soft quivering smile. "The tap dancer here named Dorothy is my sister."

"Really?"

"Really. Family is the dearest thing we have in this life, AJ. I think one day you will feel the same about your sister. And your sister will feel the same for you. Some things just take time."

How on earth did she know I was talking about Adriana?

*

After dinner, Kaylee gives us the run-down on the rest of the trip. Thank goodness this is the only place we will stay from now 'til Christmas Day, which is when we're going home. She said she tried to book the trip past Christmas, but a big group had already booked the whole castle for a wedding, so our only option was to check out on Christmas Day.

Mama said we were happy to wait and have our family Christmas with presents and grandmothers back home; we hadn't hauled all our presents to Ireland with us.

Besides, my Grandma Juliana threw a fit that we weren't spending Christmas with her and letting her cook her traditional Christmas feast. Mama promised we would save it all for her—especially the cooking part. Mama hates to cook. Mama also told us that my winning this trip for us was enough of a gift, and we should all just enjoy it and be thankful.

Kaylee says, "Tomorrow we will have the hundred-mile Ring of Kerry bus ride, and see cute farmhouses and beautiful coastlines—"

So many groans interrupt her that I think she decided right then to add, "But you will have the option of staying back at the castle, if the children have proper supervision."

"Hear, hear!" we all cheer. I thought for a minute there I was going to die. I'd much rather spend a day talking to a donkey than sitting on a bus again.

My brothers and I jump up from the table and run through the halls and back to our suite to plan a day exploring the castle. We start by making up a story about being caught as stowaways on a ship; we're brought to this castle to be put in the dungeon.

I grab the biggest suitcase I can find—Adriana's, of course—and dump all of her clothes out on her bed. It should make the perfect cargo trunk. If only it weren't pink. I drag the trunk out to the sitting room and tell JR to close it once I'm inside, just to see if I can fit in there as a stowaway. As I lower the lid, the bright pink glare inside turns to pitch black.

I hear the latch click. "Okay, that's good. Let me out."

Silence.

"JR? JR, let me out."

Nothing.

I suddenly don't like the feeling of being in here. At all. It's dark. It's small. It probably doesn't have much air.... where is my brother? Where is *anyone?* "He-e-e-l-p! Let me o-u-u-u-t of h-e-r-e!"

After what seems like *eternity,* I hear the front door open and Mama's high heels as she passes by me.

"Mama-a-a-a!" I scream. *"Let me out of here!"*

"AJ, is that you in there?"

"Yes! JR shut me in here. Can you let me out?"

"JR, did you shut your sister inside that trunk?" Mama yells, making her way toward the boys' room.

"Yes, Ma'am," I hear him answer.

"Then go let her out!"

"Yes, Ma'am."

I hear JR's feet slowly approaching.

"Open it!" I yell.

"Say please," JR replies.

"Open it this minute, JR," Mama yells.

I finally hear the click of the latches, and the lid pops open, freeing my contorted little body. "You will regret the day you did this," I warn JR, while giving him the stink eye.

"You told me to close you in. What are you mad about?"

"I said close me in for five seconds, not 'til I *die!*"

"Well, you're not dead yet now, are ya?"

I guess it was partly my fault for telling JR to close the lid on the trunk, but my curiosity just about killed the cat. If it weren't for Mama finding me in the nick of time, I probably would have died. JR would have no remorse. He'd just go on eating his Oreos like nothin' happened.

At least I had time to plan my revenge while I was stuffed inside that suitcase.

After my legs are able to straighten out again, I grab my doll Sally by the arm and take her to the bedroom to plan the perfect revenge. I got Sally when I was five years old from Aunt Genevieve, who said she was a very special heirloom passed through our Italian family. Mama says she's not so sure her sister has those facts right, 'cause she's pretty sure she saw the same doll at the local Wigwam store.

JR calls her Spooky Sally because he thinks she looks creepy, especially at night. I think she looks just like any ordinary doll during the day, with dark eyes and hair, and a mouth that makes her look like she just sucked on a sour lemon. But in the dark, I have to admit that something happens to make her look kind of eerie. Sally used to scare me so much at night that I had to put toilet paper over her face just so I could go to sleep without feeling like she was watching me.

She also has a string in her back, and she sings when you pull it. She sounds like she's singing in Chinese. One night, I hid under JR's bed with Sally. After he went to bed, I pulled Sally's string. In her weird little voice, she sang, "Twinkle, Twinkle Little Star." JR was so creeped out, he ran straight for Mama and Daddy's room, screaming like a maniac. By the time Mama got to his room and looked under his bed, Sally was the only one there.

"I knew that doll was possessed!" JR yelled. But Mama knew better. I got in big trouble.

For revenge, JR tied Sally to an inner tube behind the motorboat on Indian Lake. He spun and flipped her all over the lake while I stood on the dock screaming my head off, sure that she would fly off and drown. The good thing about Sally is that she can float…and that she can still creep out JR. After what he just did to me, I think this is a good time for payback. And this creaky, old, castle is the perfect setting— especially at night.

5

The Revenge of Sally

Sally and I head to the *Princess Parlor*, where I have my Irish costume hanging in the closet. I carefully drape my crisp white blouse around Sally like a cape, and button it up until just her head is sticking out the neck hole. Then I sneak into The *King and Queen's Suite* and grab Mama's can of stiff-hold hairspray. I turn Sally upside down and spray away 'til her hair stays straight up when I flip her right-side up. I take some of Mama's black eyeliner and line Sally's eyes so she looks like Lily Munster from The Munsters—a favorite creepy TV show of mine. Back in our room, I add a dab of Adriana's sparkling blue eye shadow, just for special effects. Standing back, she looks just the way I hoped she would—super creepy. I just have to wait until dark.

Long after dark, JR is still out exploring the castle with

Noah, and Benji and Dino are already asleep. I sneak back into the boys' room, glad that JR won't be able to turn the light on when he comes to bed. I take a bungee cord, climb onto the dresser beside JR's bed, and hook one end to the chandelier, and the other end through the tag on the neck of Sally's white gown. Sally is now suspended above JR's bed—which he probably won't notice until he climbs in and his eyes adjust to the dark. I even open the curtains so the moonlight can reflect off of her white gown. She looks like a castle ghost if I ever saw one.

I lie down on JR's bed and pretend I am him, seeing Sally floating above my head. All I can say is that if anyone ever did this to me, I would never be able to own another doll for the rest of my life. JR doesn't have the imagination I do, but I will settle for just a really good scream.

I find JR and Noah by the silver knight display in the hallway. "Hey JR, isn't it about time to hit the hay?"

"Why? What's it to ya?" he says back.

"I was just thinkin', you gotta get up early if you plan to do the Pirate's Plunge into the moat tomorrow." That's another plan the boys came up with that they haven't run by Mama.

He gives me the *mind your own business* glare and goes back to checking out the armory on the knights.

Right then, Noah's mama pops her head out of their suite. "Time for bed, Noah!" she calls from the west wing.

Nice timing.

By the time JR finally goes to brush his teeth, the entire family is sound asleep except for me. Daddy is snoring. Adriana is asleep with her head full of sponge curlers and her beauty eye-shades on, looking creepier than Sally.

I decide the best place for me to be when JR encounters Spooky Sally is lying in my bed, preferably asleep, because then I will get the full thrill, along with the rest of the family, when JR wakes us up screaming.

I quietly slip into my canopy bed and lie as still as possible, hoping to fall asleep before JR climbs into bed. Unfortunately, my mind knows what I am up to. It won't let me trick myself into pretending this is any other ordinary night where nothing exciting is about to happen that will blast us all out of our deep, sweet sleep.

As I'm getting frustrated with not being able to trick myself, I hear JR shuffle down the hall to his room. My entire body begins to shake with anticipation. I wait....and shake....and wait...and wait some more. Nothing. Absolutely nothing. My body slowly relaxes in total and utter defeat. Drat.

Hours later ....

"Auuuuugggggghhhhhh!"

I bolt upright. My eyes dart around the room in sheer terror. The clock says 1:00 a.m.

"What the *heck?*" Adriana yells from the bed next to me, and whips her eye-shades right off her sponge-curled head. I hear Daddy jump to the floor as the twins start to scream along with JR. A light flashes on in the hallway, and the sound of other doors echo through the castle walls. Someone knocks on our suite door, and Mama goes to answer it.

Meanwhile, Daddy opens JR's door. *Three, two, one…*

"AJ!"

"Yes, Daddy?"

"Get in here!"

*

6

JR's Revenge

"Mama, have you seen Sally?"

"Not since she was hovering over your brother's bed last night, waking up the entire castle. I wouldn't be surprised if the management banished her to the dungeon for haunting their guests." Mama goes back to reading her newspaper.

I have a feeling someone is up to foul play where Sally is concerned, and his initials are JR. I was not given a chance to go back for her last night. After Daddy got a hold of me, I was banished to my room until he could come back and lecture me good this morning. It had something to do with how my actions of revenge punished more people than just my intended victim, and if I were wise, I would learn how to call a truce with my enemy before it goes any further. What Daddy doesn't realize, is, when it comes to me and JR, there is no such thing as a truce. There's also a very high likelihood that JR's revenge on me is already in progress. I head downstairs to investigate.

"Hey, AJ," Benji runs through the lobby to meet me. "You'd better get out to the moat if you ever want to see Sally again!"

What? I run out the front door to the bridge that crosses the moat. "Sally!" I scream at the top of my lungs. My poor doll is floating, face down, in the slimy waters of the moat. The water is so green with algae it looks like a lime Jell-O mold surrounding the castle.

I can hear JR and Dino laughing on the other side of the moat.

"JR! You get Sally out of there! She's going to fill up and sink!" I scream across the water.

"She's fine. She was the only one brave enough to do the Pirate's Plunge. Now she's working on her crawl stroke."

I run over and grab an oar from the rowboat on shore

and stand on the bridge over the moat, waiting for Sally to float by so I can drag her back to shore. The moat is only about twenty feet across, like a deep stream, so it shouldn't be too hard to reach her. If only the wind would kick up and push her along.

"Why did you bring that ugly doll to Ireland, anyway?" JR yells. "Aren't you a little old for playing with dolls?"

"I didn't bring her to play with! I brought her to get her an Irish outfit, you creep. I'm saving her for when I have my own kids. Now her hair will be ruined forever!"

"Her hair was already ruined. You had enough hairspray in there to last her a lifetime—I'm just trying to wash it out." The boys laugh like that is just so funny. "I can't believe you'd want to creep your own kids out with such an ugly doll!"

After waiting on the bridge for a good ten minutes, Sally finally floats within my oar's reach and I guide her back to shore while crossing the bridge. Poor Sally. I can hardly imagine how many stories she will have by the time I have kids. She probably won't have any hair or eyes left by then. All the more endearing—she'll be like The Velveteen Rabbit. Kind of.

After laying Sally out to dry by the fireplace in our suite, I head down the hall to snoop around the rest of this Baby Blarney castle. Besides the two suites upstairs, there are six smaller rooms on the ground level. Our family and Noah's family got the two biggest suites, and all the tappers are sharing the ground floor rooms. The banquet room and library are also on the ground floor, as well as a small gift shop. There are pictures of grumpy-looking men in uniforms and sour-faced women up and down all of the walls. It looks like they didn't have much fun here in the olden days.

Wandering down a long corridor, I hear the sound of toe-tapping from inside the castle library. Peeking inside, I realize Tina's Tappers are in the middle of a dress rehearsal—probably for their surprise performance. I'm putting my money on it being tonight at the *medieval banquet.* According to Kaylee, the kitchen workers will all be dressed up like scullery maids and servants. She said we could dress up, too, but I want to save my fancy Irish costume for whenever we get to make our surprise performance. I don't want anyone to think, "Yeah, yeah, seen it already." The real surprise will be what we will be doing besides just standing there. It's not like we have any special skills or anything. All we have to show are our Irish outfits—that's not much of a performance if you ask me.

I'm still on the hunt for Sally's matching Irish doll outfit. I haven't really done much looking yet. My only hope left is either at the souvenir shop at the big Blarney Castle or at the small gift shop here.

Tina catches me spying and motions for me to come inside. "Come join us, AJ!" she calls. I slip in and sit down to watch. The women are all in green, sequined vests and red top hats, and they're carrying little white canes. Netti is sitting on the side, so I go and sit beside her.

Netti says she isn't feeling up to snuff and doesn't think she's going to be able to perform. "The gals really need twelve dancers to do this number right, but I just can't seem to shake this cough."

Rockin' Around the Christmas Tree is blaring away from a phonograph, and all of their toes are tapping like crazy to the beat. "I think I learned this dance in my tap class," I mention to Netti.

"You know how to tap?" Netti's eyes light up.

"A little. I had two years of lessons before my tapping drove my whole family crazy. I had to quit before Mama moved out."

Netti stands up and whistles to the team, "Ladies! AJ knows tap! She can take my place tonight in the show!"

Before I know it, I am swept off my chair and pulled into the middle of the group. "I'm going to coach her," Dolly announces. "You have two hours to learn the routine," she says to me.

No pressure.

It's a good thing Netti is so little, because they pull her tap shoes right off of her feet and put them on mine—with two cotton balls stuffed into the toes first. Then Annie takes Netti's sequined vest and hat and dresses me like I'm her little doll. The second Annie shoves a little cane in my hand, Dolly whisks me off to the side of the room and starts going over the steps with me. The routine is a little bit different from the one I learned, but not by much. Before long, I am placed in line beside Dorothy and Betty, and I stumble my way through the dance with them. Tina told me to keep it a secret from everyone else, so it would be a double surprise when we perform tonight at the banquet. *Boy, will it ever!*

When I return to our suite, Sally's hair is dry and she looks back to her old weird self again. Mama and Daddy are sitting by the fireplace reading.

"Where ya been, kiddo?" Mama asks.

"Oh, just exploring."

"See anything interesting?" Daddy asks.

Yep. But I can't talk about it or it won't be a surprise."

Mama and Daddy look at each other with a hint of concern, but go back to reading.

"Where's Adriana?" I ask, as I grab Sally.

"She said she was going to find you," Mama says. "That was quite a while ago."

I knew it. She's with Yodel Boy. She always uses me as the decoy when it comes to boys. Mama and Daddy should know by now I'm the last person on earth Adriana would want to find right now.

Sally and I take the big grand staircase down to the lobby and look at the gift shop window display. The only Irish doll outfits are on dolls half the size of Sally. But I do spot a stuffed bear about her size, and it's wearing a blue and green plaid dress. I go inside to check it out. It looks a little big for Sally, but it could work if it had to.

"Can I help ye, little miss?" the shop lady asks.

"Well, I'm looking for an outfit for my doll. That one looks like it might fit, but would I have to buy the whole bear to get it?"

"Well, let me see now," the lady says. "It does look a wee bit big, but I think we might be able to finagle your dolly into it. It's a mighty bonnie little dress for your bonnie little doll."

"Her name isn't Bonnie," I tell her politely. "It's Sally."

The shop lady smiles. "Bonnie is just our way of saying something is pretty."

"Ahhh." I add that to my list of words I know in Irish.

"Now, as for the outfit, it does come with the bear. Do you suppose you might have someone you could give the bear to for Christmas?"

"Hey, that's a good idea. My little brothers like bears. They would never know it was a girl bear if I took the dress off. All I'd have to do is make a little sword for him, and they'd think it was a boy bear for sure. I could make him into a warrior bear."

"My, that's some imagination ye have there. Ye know, we have a little Viking sword here you might like to buy to go with it. We could put it right in the little bear's hand, like so." She puts the bear's paw through the handle. It's a perfect fit—although it looks funny with a sword and a dress at the same time, like a girl warrior bear.

"I love it!" I tell her. "Then, when they fight over it, one can have the bear the other can have the sword. But, the thing is, I didn't bring my money with me. My sister's keeping it for me in her purse, but she's gone right now." I have no idea how much this bear costs because it's all in shillings here. But I brought my whole years' worth of allowance and birthday money with me, so I should be okay.

"Not a problem at all, little miss. You just tell me the number of your suite, and I can put it on your room charge.

You can pay it at the end of your stay."

"Oh, that would be great. I'll take the bear and the sword. Could we take the dress off first?"

The nice lady wraps the dress separately for me in tissue, and puts the bear into a big gift box with a bow. Now I just have to smuggle it into my room with no one seeing it. Won't everyone be surprised when they see this bear on Christmas morning?

Once I'm safely back in my room, I hide the bear in the closet, then try the outfit on Sally. It is so cute! It looks a little like a hand-me-down 'cause it's kinda big; like when I get one of Adriana's old dresses that I haven't quite grown into yet. That's okay. People can just think Sally has a big sister who gave her the dress.

7

Rockin' Around the Christmas Tree

Walking into the dining room is like stepping into a castle ballroom a thousand years ago; Sugar Shamrocks brought in a theater group and made everything look just like medieval times. The real lights are turned off, and there are torches flaming from the walls, and a giant chandelier of candles hanging from the ceiling. Our long, long table is decked out to the nines.

The "king" is seated at the head in his kingly knickers, and the "queen" is in the fanciest ball gown I have ever seen. It even out-does Cousin Stacy's *Gone With the Wind* get-up. A fancy butler escorts us to our seats at the table, which is full of gold plates, goblets, and a glowing candelabra in the middle of the table.

I feel a little out of place in my denim overalls, but I want everyone to notice the dramatic change when I appear in all my sequins after dinner. Adriana, on the other hand, wants everyone to notice her before, during, and after dinner. She's all done up in a hot pink miniskirt and high heels. I'm pretty sure there was no such color as hot pink in the medieval days, because she is the only one here wearing that color. Hans took a night off from his yodeling costume—probably so Adriana wouldn't be embarrassed to sit by him, because she would be. It seems to have worked. Noah comes over and sits with me and JR while the twins are busy trying to climb the castle wall using the drapes—until Daddy yanks them back down to earth.

Mama looks 'faboo' as always. That's Mama's word for fabulous. She pulled off a perfect Sophia Loren tonight; bouffant hairdo, swooshy black eyeliner, bright red dress and Red Lady lipstick, but the Irish don't seem to know who Miss Loren is. No one has asked for her autograph yet. I'm sure some of Tina's Tappers would notice, but they haven't arrived yet. They're probably getting things set up for the grand finale.

While everyone is getting settled, some pied pipers

come prancing through the dining hall playing flutes and fiddles. These must be the king's merry men! I have *always* wanted to see these happy little jesters that show up in old movies. With leaps and jumps, they weave around our table like delightful little elves playing wonderful Christmas music.

Suddenly, one of the merry men grabs me by the hand and pulls me into line with them. The others grab Benji, Dino, and Noah—they seem to know better than to touch the bigger kids like JR or Adriana—they can give a look that says "Don't even think about it."

I'm skipping along with the music, whirling and twirling, and having a merry ol' time...until I crash into the suit of armor that's standing guard along the wall, and I knock his head off. His helmet crashes to the ground and echoes so loudly that everyone stops to see what on earth just happened. It's a good thing the lights aren't on in here, because my face lights up like a torch whenever I am this embarrassed. I decide not to even look at Adriana. I can imagine the dramatic eye roll. But that same little merry man grabs my hand and pulls me back into the action. The music starts back up, and everyone just forgets about what a klutz I am.

"Smooth move, AJ."

Well, almost everyone. My sister doesn't count.

While I'm being whirled around the room, feeling like I'm the end player in a game of Crack the Whip, a huge platter of food comes sailing out of the kitchen, carried by two scullery maids, and I'm headed right for it. Thankfully I fly right past the platter of food and avoid splattering roast boar all over the room.

The king pierces the roast with his knife and nods in approval. The queen takes a sip of wine from the goblet she is handed and nods her approval, as well. Then a whole team of servants stream in with plates and bowls and platters of food and serve us, the royal guests of honor.

After our five-course meal, they announce the figgy pudding. I am so full, I'm about to burst...and I have to tap dance soon, so I decide to pass on dessert. Besides, I'm pretty sure figgy is just a fancy word for prunes.

Tina taps me on the shoulder from behind and whispers, "It's time, sweetheart."

While the guests are all raving over the food, I slip out without knocking anything else over and sneak backstage. The tappers are putting on their sequins and tap shoes; Netti helps me with mine. "You go out there and dance your little heart out for me!"

"I will," I tell her, as I find my place on the stage. Once Tina nods, the big velvet curtain slowly raises up, and the guests turn their attention to us. *Rockin' Around the Christmas Tree* begins to play on the phonograph player, and my feet start moving. Before I know it, I am tapping my way across the stage with the best of them.

Catching a quick glance of my audience; Mama and Daddy look surprised; Adriana looks annoyed. My shuffle steps are a little rusty at first, but by the second half of the song, I'm up to speed. We all wave our hats as we kick to the right, then raise our canes as we kick to the left. I get most of those moves right. I get a little tangled up in the grapevine, but come back to my shuffle steps pretty good. We have a nice slow eight counts of the shuffle step-step-steps, then, the grand finale comes.

We all form a conga-line to do a shuffle–hop-step routine. My little legs can't hop as high as theirs, but I'm giving it my all. After three good shuffle-hop-steps, instead of doing my shuffle, then my hop, I do them both at the same time; leap in the air while shuffling forward, causing me to fling backwards into Dorothy, which causes Dorothy to fall backwards into Annie. Annie falls into Dolly, and Dolly falls into Marilyn, and Marilyn falls into Marjorie, and Marjorie falls into Wilma, and Wilma falls into Pam, and Pam falls into Mary, and Mary falls into Angie...right down the line, like dominoes.

I slowly raise my head, hoping it's all just a nightmare, but quickly realize, it's not. Hats and canes and sequined tappers are lying all over the stage. I'm so horrified, I jump up to bolt off the stage, but my foot catches on the phonograph cord and I fly head first, skidding across the stage, then drop in slow motion into the orchestra pit.

Rockin' Around the Christmas Tree continues to play on in the background as though nothing has happened. Instead of getting up, I decide to just lie here. Maybe if they think I'm dead, they won't be as upset with me for ruining the show.

*

After a fitful night's sleep, I hobble into the dining room for breakfast, with my elbows and knees covered in Band-Aids. Nobody says a word to me about me *Rockin' Around the Christmas Tree,* except Mama. "Hey, you looked faboo last night in your sequins and sparkle, kiddo."

The boys start snickering. "Yeah, right up 'til you fell off the ...."

Mama gives Dino *the look.*

"Uh…nice sequins, AJ," he says.

Mama must have given the boys the gag order. I tell myself *no one will remember this in five years.* It's a phrase that works with most things I botch up. After all, when I think five years back, to when I was four, the only embarrassing thing I remember is wiping out on my bicycle and skidding through the intersection of Durlin and Exiter on my face, in front of a million cars. It was my first victory ride without training wheels. The main reason I remember *that* is because I broke my collarbone and got stitches in my head, and it hurt like the dickens. But I'm sure I must have done other embarrassing things I can't remember, so that's how I know the *five years from now* thing works.

"Good morning, *Grace,*" Adriana says to me when she arrives at the table.

Mama waits until Adriana sits down and quietly says, "I vaguely remember you asking your father if you could go to a New Year's party when we get home."

"What's that got to do with anything?" Adriana shoots back.

"As I recall," Mama says, "his answer was, 'It's up to your mother.'"

That's Mama's way of strongly suggesting that Adriana had better watch her tongue.

"What's the plan for today?" Daddy asks.

Mama looks at the flyer that came with breakfast this morning; "Free time until this afternoon. Then we are all heading to a folk festival to see traditional Irish dancing."

"I'm too busy to go. I need to do my nails," Adriana protests.

"Great," Daddy says. "Bring your nail file with you."

Adriana glares at me instead of Daddy. Why am I the *escape goat* for everything? It's only obvious she wants to stay here and sneak off with her storybook hero, Hansel. Sadly, for Hans, Adriana's fairytale would have a creepy twist; by the time the two of them reach the little cottage in the woods, Hans will realize that Adriana is really the wicked witch instead of sweet Gretel.

"There is no way I can wash *and* set my hair, *and* change my nail polish in time to go this afternoon. I'd rather stay here than wear this red nail polish with the skirt I'm planning to wear. People notice things like that."

Rather than listen to Adriana, I take my breakfast biscuits out to share with Paddy. He's much better company than a delusional teenager.

While I'm sitting on the rock wall, I notice that Paddy's back is only inches below where I'm sitting. If I were to slowly lower myself down, and slide one leg over his back....like so....

Paddy jolts away from the wall with me on his back. I squeeze my legs to keep from falling off, but that makes him go faster, and he takes off running like the horse in *National Velvet*. But I can't ride like Elizabeth Taylor! At least, not without a saddle and reins!

"He-e-e-lp!" I'm screaming, holding on to Paddy's neck for dear life. When I get enough courage to open my eyes, the only thing I see is a low-hanging willow branch coming at me. "N-n-n-n-ooooo!!"

Wack!

I hit the ground with a thud. Paddy's not very tall, but I land hard enough to knock the wind out of myself. I'm gasping for air and waiting for my brains to settle back down when a big muzzle lowers and blows warm donkey breath in my face.

"Hi, Paddy. I hope you're the only one that saw that."

Paddy and I hobble back to the stable together. It's a good thing my elbows and knees were already protected with Band-Aids. Something about this feels like a double déjà vu. First, falling off the stage, then the fairy tale I told Netti. But *Adriana* was supposed to be the mean step sister on the runaway donkey—not me.

When you fall off a donkey and nobody sees, does it even count as a blunder?

*

The folk festival is in a grand old theater full of people from all over. I can tell by all the different hats. All the lights are out, and I can hardly find my way to my seat. The seats are the hard wooden kind that you fold down. We are only six rows from the stage—a very high stage—the kind you would not want to fall off of.

As soon as we take our seats, a dim light shines down on the stage, and gets brighter and brighter. I soon realize that the stage is full of dancers wearing black, holding very still. Then the music starts up, real slow at first, but building up into a fast frenzy. There are feet flying all over the stage with very loud taps. But these taps are double taps—they jingle, like two taps clanging together every move they make.

Clogging is different from tap. These dancers hold their hands down at their sides. In tap, our arms move up, and out, and forward with the dance steps. Irish dance is all about the feet. This is what Tina's Tappers are hoping to learn while they're here. I guess the best way to learn it is to try and tap along with them and see if I can pick up the rhythm.

My toes start to tap along with the music, until I get Adriana's elbow in my arm.

After a few minutes, I try making really small, quiet taps.

Another elbow.

This time, I wait about five minutes, then I barely move my toes up and down inside my shoes and slowly work my way up....

Adriana's spiked high heel comes smashing down on top of my foot.

"*O-u-u-u-ch!*" I yell so loud that people in all five rows in front of us turn around to see what happened. I turn around, too, and pretend it was someone in the row behind me.

*

After returning to the castle, I climb into my pajamas and limp my way to Mama and Daddy's bedroom to say goodnight. Daddy's already asleep, but Mama is sitting up in bed reading *Doctor Zhivago*.

"What's with the limp?" Mama asks, peering over the top of her book. "Still a little sore from *Rockin' Around the Christmas Tree?*"

"You mean rockin' off the end of the stage?"

Mama smiles. "You'll grow into your feet soon enough, kiddo."

"Not if Adriana keeps smashing my feet with her spiked high heels. That's what I'm limping from this time."

Mama pats a spot on the blanket beside her, so I hop up on the big bed and join her. "Did she accidently step on you?"

"Accidently? Mama, no injuries from Adriana are accidental. She was trying to stop me from tapping along with the cloggers. I got two elbow jabs and a foot stomp by the time it was over."

Mama puts her book down and looks down at me. "You know, AJ, your Aunt Genevieve and I didn't get along much better than the two of you when we were kids. I know older sisters can be kind of tough on little sisters at times."

"Kind of?"

"Still, sisters have a way of becoming good friends when they get older."

"That's what Netti just told me."

"Well, I think Netti may be right."

"But how can you stand all of Adriana's sass— I mean, I'm a kid and I can't even stand it."

Mama laughs. "I have a special memory that gets me

through almost anything you kids throw at me."

"You do? Can you tell me what it is?" I lean my head on Mama's shoulder.

Mama sighs. "I suppose I could." She puts her arm around me and begins... "One very rainy day, shortly after you were born, I was extremely tired. I had three young kids at home and was dying for a nap. So, I gathered up all three of you; you, JR, and Adriana, and brought you in bed with me. I was laying on my back with you on my tummy, JR on my right side, and Adriana on my left. I told JR and Adriana we were playing a special rain game; we all needed to lie as still as possible, close our eyes, and listen to the rain on the roof without saying a word. I told them God was sending us a sweet, gentle rain lullaby. Do you know what my next memory was?"

"No, what?" I whisper.

"Waking up; with you asleep on my tummy, Adriana asleep in one arm, and JR asleep in my other. All I could hear was that rain on the roof and the soft, sweet breathing of my three babies'. I was holding my whole world in my arms; and I knew I would never have another moment that precious as long as I lived."

"So how does that help you when Adriana's sneering at you and sassing her head off?"

Mama smiles down at me. "No matter how old my babies get, you will always be my babies. When Adriana is sneering at me and sassing her head off, somehow that snotty-faced teenager turns into that sweet little girl with the face of an angel, asleep in my arms. That's what I see when I look at her, and that's what gets me through."

"Wow. You must have a really good imagination, Mama."

8

A Bunch of Blarney

"You can't be serious," Adriana moans. *"This* is what everyone comes to Ireland for?"

We're visiting the big Blarney Castle, with its 125 stone steps that spiral straight up to the top, where the infamous Blarney Stone resides. Adriana's commentary follows me up the entire staircase. "When they said *castle,* I pictured a *palace,* not a stone-cold tower of *rock.* I can't believe royalty actually lived like this! No carpet, no electricity…these rooms are smaller than my bedroom. And I'm not even a princess."

That's debatable.

Once we've huffed and puffed our way to the top, we emerge onto a castle rooftop under an open sky. It is way high up here. Kaylee explains that the reason people kiss the Blarney Stone is for the gift of gab.

"Oh, great," Adriana moans. "Just what AJ needs to drive us all the way insane. Keep my sister away from that stone—we still have to live with her for the rest of our lives."

"Very funny," I reply and march into line behind the other brave souls.

"Wait!" Adriana snaps. "What are those people doing—they're hanging over the edge of the castle backwards!"

"That's how you kiss the stone," Kaylee replies.

My eyes zoom in on the famous Blarney Stone that I've waited so long to see. *That's* the Blarney Stone? I have to say, I feel a twinge of disappointment at first glance. I was kind of expecting it to be a huge shiny jewel; a *precious* stone, like a jumbo ruby or something. It's actually just a big square bluish-gray rock with no sparkle. But, I still want to kiss it. I remind myself how old and special it is to all these people…except Adriana.

"I can't believe they are all kissing that ugly stone, upside down. That's crazy dangerous…and think of all the germs on that stone! Eww."

Kaylee tries to reassure her. "Don't worry, dear, they wipe it clean after each kiss."

"That's disgusting!" Adriana scowls. "This whole thing is nuts. And who wants the gift of gab, anyway? Maybe if it were the Fountain of Youth I'd risk my life, but for the gift of talking as much as AJ? Forget it. I'm out of here!" Adriana turns and makes a hasty exit back to the staircase.

I, on the other hand, lie on my back as instructed, do a backbend over the edge, and pucker up.

"I hope we don't have an earthquake up here," Benji says, just as I'm kissing the stone.

The thought of the castle crumbling beneath me while I'm hanging upside down, makes me suddenly light-headed and I feel like I'm going to....

"AJ? AJ!"

It's Mama's voice that I hear from a distant land as I slowly regain consciousness. I find myself lying flat on the cold stone floor, staring up at a gray sky overhead.

"AJ," Daddy says. "Are you with us?"

"Huh? What happened?"

"Well, kiddo, you fainted when you were kissing the stone," Mama explains.

"Yeah, it took two big Irishmen—one on each side of you to hoist you back up so you wouldn't slither down the castle wall and smash to the ground four stories down."

"Thanks," I groan, remembering it was his earthquake comment that made me dizzy in the first place. I turn my head away as a wave of despair washes over me.

"AJ, what's wrong? Why are you crying?" Mama leans over me.

"Does this mean I won't get the g-gift of g-gab?"

"Believe me, you have nothing to worry about," Mama reassures me. "You kissed the stone before you fainted. You're good to go."

I decide I'm ready to have my feet back on solid ground. As I'm heading for the stairs, I hear Mama whisper to Daddy, "If there's such a thing as an overdose of the gift of gab—she just got it."

When I reach ground level, I find Adriana wandering along the path back toward the restaurant. There are a few teenage boys following her, and Adriana's pretending not to notice. Nothing new there.

"Adriana," I run up to her. "Guess what happened? I was leaning back, kissing the Blarney Stone, and I suddenly got really dizzy, and—"

"AJ! Thanks a lot. You just scared off two incredibly handsome guys with your *ridiculous* Blarney babble. They were just about to buy me lunch!"

I glance at the two guys, who are now walking the other direction. I actually saved them from the oldest trick in Adriana's book. She would have walked into the restaurant, stopped to look helplessly around before making eye contact with them. Then, she would smile and say something charming, like, "I feel kind of silly asking for a table for one...." And the guys would say, "Oh, please, join us." And before they know it, when the tab comes, they're saying, "No, allow us to take care of that." It's the old *save the helpless damsel in distress* trick.

My sister is so obvious; I can't believe guys fall for this over and over—all over the world.

9

A Midnight Clear

We were secretly informed by Kaylee, after returning to Baby Blarney, that tonight would be our family presentation night. I think everyone but me was hoping Kaylee had forgotten about us. Adriana says I've got "a snowball's chance in Tucson" of getting her back into that tacky jumper again.

Not only did Kaylee say, "I can't wait to see all of you in your Irish outfits," but she also told us that since we don't yodel or tap dance, we get to sing some of our traditional American Christmas Carols. Nobody in our family is musically inclined and will not be happy about singing in public. *At all.* This could be very awkward.

Personally, I can't wait to dress up Irish, especially since Sally will be with me in her new Irish outfit, too. I think about how easy it was to say "put it on my room charge," which gives me a great idea. Since no one is expecting to get Christmas presents here, wouldn't it be fun to play Secret St. Nicholas and get presents for the whole family?

No one will know who they came from. It will be like having a wee little Christmas after all.

*

Irish Rover; Christmas Eve 1967

There was a different shopkeeper working the gift shop today. She was fine with me charging everything to my room after I told her the other lady let me. She even gift-wrapped all the presents for me. Won't everyone be surprised when they find these mysterious gifts on Christmas morning? I even bought one for myself—I had to, just so they wouldn't figure out it was me who gave the gifts to everyone. It would be a dead giveaway if I was the only one without a present. Besides, they had the most adorable little musical teapot with an entire mouse family living inside of it, all wearing tiny Christmas outfits, having tea with ultra-miniature tea cups, and cookies the size of sequins with sprinkles on top!

*

Sneaking around the *Princess Parlor* to hide my gift boxes, I hear Mama's voice in the other room; "No, JR, you cannot fake sick to get out of it." And, "Just put on the dress and deal with it, Adriana. It's the price we all pay for a free trip to Ireland."

"It's the price we all pay for having a sister like AJ," JR

replies.

My Christmas spirit begins to plummet as I stash all the gifts in the closet. *Doesn't anyone appreciate this trip? Would they rather be at home than here in a castle?*

"I'd rather be at home than here in this dumb castle wearing a dumb skirt," JR adds.

Well, I guess that answers it.

I don't care what they think. I am going to have the best night of my life, with or without my family. I grab my dress off the hanger and get Sally's outfit laid out for her on the bed. "Sally, it's you and me tonight—we are going to party and sing and have the time of our lives. *Sally?* Sally, where are you?"

I stick my head out into the sitting room, "Anyone here seen Sally?"

Dino and Benji look at each other guiltily. "I'll get her," Dino says. He returns with Sally, who is blindfolded and has her hands tied behind her back. Her hair is a mess and her dress is all wrinkled. "We needed to use her as a Viking prisoner of war in our battle today." He tosses her back to me.

Great. Now there are two of us who need complete makeovers before dinner.

*

Sally and I arrive at dinner in our matching plaid dresses. Dino and Benji are already seated in their cute little plaid kilts and green vests. Daddy is sporting his kilt and green knee-highs with that pretend smile that he has whenever we go to the cousins' house. It's tough on a six foot tall park ranger like Daddy to wear a kilt. He is giving it his best shot, but is not thrilled. That's pure love.

Mama strides in with her head held high. She knows she can pull off anything she has to, even a long plaid jumper with an apron. Mama knows how to accessorize when she needs to, and she has accessorized to the hilt! JR trails behind her without even making the effort not to look miserable. The only one missing is Adriana.

The Yodel family went all out and wore their Hansel knickers and Gretel dresses, complete with red and green Christmas trim. Except for Hans, who is in a pair of jeans. The rebel.

Tonight's Christmas Eve menu is displayed on fancy paper at each place setting:

~AN IRISH CHRISTMAS EVE FEAST ~

Cream of potato soup and crackers

Roast goose or wild salmon in basil cream

Creamed peas and potatoes

Scalloped potatoes with leeks

Brown bread

Christmas rum punch

Irish Christmas cake

Plum Pudding

"Do you think Adriana will be in our presentation, Mama?" I ask hesitantly. *She can't blow our only chance to be on the cover of Sugar Shamrocks.*

"Yes, she will be there."

"How do you know?"

"Because I told her if she wanted to stay out past 8:30 on New Year's Eve, she'd better jump into the jumper."

Mama knows exactly what tricks to pull on each one of us when she has to.

Just as the waiters are bringing us little crocks of soup, Adriana struts in, wearing what used to be a long, plaid, Irish jumper. It is now an Irish mini-jumper with fishnet stockings and black, patent-leather high heels.

Everyone is looking at her. Most of them look

shocked; Hans looks pleased. My family barely reacts. We have learned to just ignore her cries for attention, and move on with life.

"Please pass the crackers."

*

Irish feasts have all kinds of potatoes: smashed, scalloped, roasted, and creamed. These people sure love their spuds!

After a few bites of dinner, I have one of each of the desserts. The Christmas cake is really fruitcake in disguise. Something about green cherries just doesn't work for me. And I'm suspicious that plum pudding is just another secret name for prune pudding; adults are always looking for tricks to get kids to eat things. I decide to go back to potatoes when Kaylee gives us the "You're on" signal.

My family reluctantly scoots out their chairs and follows me and Sally to the front of the dining room. Kaylee gets everyone's attention by ringing a little Christmas bell.

"Well, we have our final performance tonight with the Degulio family, dressed in wonderful Irish costumes handmade by AJ and her grandmother."

I thought about telling them that I only sewed on the buttons, but Kaylee was busy flashing a photo of us, so decided to just smile big and go with it.

"For their special presentation, I've asked them to sing us a few American Christmas carols, which I'm sure you will know, so feel free to join in with them. I've asked AJ to pick the songs that she grew up with. So, with no further ado, let's give a listen to the Degulio family carolers!"

My entire family is staring at me, waiting to hear what songs I've chosen. I forgot to discuss that part with them, for fear that none of them would come. It was enough of a challenge just getting them all here in the costumes. "Well, our first number is one that has always been our family favorite, called *Jolly Old Saint Nicholas.*"

Rather than wait for my family to join me, I just clutch

Sally in front of my chest for security and belt out the words as loud as I can.

"Jolly old Saint Nicholas, lean your ear this way, don't you tell a single soul, what I'm going to say..."

Thank goodness Tina's Tappers know the words and join right in, because my family is acting like they've never heard this song before in their lives.

Our next song is *Silent Night,* which is fitting, because most of my family remains silent. Again, audience participation is my only relief.

For the last song, I decide to put my family on the spot and tell them they get to choose the song. After an awkward moment, Benji and Dino save the day by offering to do a duet of *Silver Bells* in the voices of Alvin and the Chipmunks. The rest of the Degulios abandon the stage as fast as rats abandoning a sinking ship.

Swaying back and forth in their little kilts and vests, Dino and Benji do a perfect imitation of high-pitched chipmunk voices. The audience cheers. The boys are so encouraged that they launch into *The Twelve Days of Christmas,* making up all the things "my true love gave to me." There are two silver swords, three crumbling castles, four Blarney Stones, five Paddy's piping, six leprechauns leaping, seven courageous Celtics ....on and on...and a Viking in a pear tree.

By the end of the song, everyone is cheering and laughing so hard that I sigh with relief, knowing that my brothers saved us from our completely botched performance.

Dino and Benji are busy signing autographs on the dinner menus that JR and Noah bring them...probably hoping they can sell them to the audience.

Adriana, in her Irish mini-glam-girl outfit, goes off with Mr. blue-jeans-yodeler to a table of their own. The little rebels are too cool to sit with any of us "ridiculous" people.

Mama and Daddy toast each other with tall glasses of

rum punch, looking relieved it's over. *"Slante!"*

*

Candlelight Nativity

Kaylee announces that anyone who wishes to attend the midnight candlelight vigil at St. Nicholas Church can go on the Blarney Bus. Our family has always gone to the Christmas Eve vigil at home, and Mama says we'll continue that tradition here in Ireland. We all need to find a good way to kill time between now and 11:00 p.m.

I want to spend my time with Paddy under the starry sky, just like the shepherds abiding in their fields on Christmas Eve. After changing back into my overalls, I tell Mama they can find me in the same place they could have found Baby Jesus on Christmas. I don't explain that means down at the stable; I just leave them with the clue.

Slipping out the front door of the castle, I am greeted by the starry night and frosty air. My breath comes back out like a puff of smoke. The only sound I hear is Paddy walking from the pasture to the stable. I follow the sound of his footsteps until I can see his breath as a puff of smoke, just like mine. When I'm climbing over the rock wall, he comes to greet me. His breath feels warm on my hands as he sniffs around in search of the Christmas carrot I snagged for him in the dining room. His crunching of each bite is earth-shatteringly loud out here.

There is something tingly about being alone in the night with a donkey on Christmas Eve. I think of the shepherds, and the angels, and the cattle lowing, and Baby Jesus, and heaven and nature singing.

When people say they don't believe in God because they can't see Him, all I can think is they must have never stood outside, under the stars, on Christmas Eve with a donkey.

*

The candles in the midnight nativity service are like the stars in that dark sky above Paddy's pasture, whispering, *"Holy, Holy, Holy,"* with the whole universe echoing, *"Glory to God in the highest."*

10

A Wee Little Christmas

"Joy to the world, the Lord is come!"

"Go back to bed, you nutcase," Adriana grumbles.

Not everyone gets as excited as I do about Christmas morning—especially the ones who aren't morning people.

I know I can get the twins to rally; they are always looking for an excuse to get out of bed, any hour of the day or night. "Hey, check out all the presents under the tree!"

Kaylee surprised us by putting a miniature Christmas tree in our suite while we were at church last night. We came home and there it was in our sitting room—a tiny green tree with twinkle lights. Maybe it's an Irish tradition to put a tree

up on Christmas Eve, 'cause there was also a giant tree all

lit up in the lobby when we came home from church after

midnight.

The boys run out to see what's under the tree.

They're surprised that there is anything at all, since Mama

keeps telling them we're postponing our Christmas gifts.

"Wow! They all have names on 'em, too!"

It's so fun to play Secret St. Nicholas. Most people

play "Secret Santa," but I like that St. Nicholas was a real

person.

When I was little, I never could figure out how Santa

got down the chimney if he was so fat. Then, when I found

out he wasn't real, I was crushed for weeks. When my

parents added the Tooth Fairy and Easter Bunny to the list

of "not real," I really went over the edge. I couldn't trust

anyone anymore. One night, when I was about six, I was

staring at Mama and Daddy at dinner, and Mama said, "AJ,

why are you looking at us so funny?"

I cocked my head to one side, and said, "I was just trying to figure out if you and Daddy are real."

That's when Mama decided to take me to the priest for help. Even though he told me that the fat Santa with the flying reindeer wasn't real, he explained that there really was a St. Nicholas who loved children and gave gifts to poor people. I finally snapped out of it. I wasn't so worried about the Tooth Fairy, 'cause I'd already lost most of my teeth and made a bundle off her before I found out she wasn't real.

Watching my brothers, I can't wait for everyone to try to guess where all these gifts came from. I'm never going to tell. I plan to pay off my charge at the front desk before we leave. *My twenty-five bucks will be enough to cover it.*

"Hey, Benji, go pull Mama and Daddy out of bed." They'll think it's cute if the boys do it. I'm too old for them to think it's cute anymore.

By the time the sun comes up, Mama and Daddy are

on their second cup of coffee each, and the kids are sipping cocoa, waiting impatiently for Adriana to drag herself from her beauty rest to join us.

Finally, my sister grumbles her way to the couch and wraps herself up in a blanket.

"Can we start now?" the twins yell.

"Well, first," Mama says, "since we all agreed that we weren't doing gifts here, I'm curious why there are gifts after all?"

Nobody answers.

I even had the shop lady write the names on the gift tags so no one would recognize my handwriting. I just wander over and start reading the tags like I'm just as puzzled as everyone else about this. "Mama, look, this is for you." I hand her the little box, gift-wrapped in shiny gold paper from the *Blarney Beag Boutique.*

Mama slowly unties the ribbon, opens the lid of the

box, and gasps. "Oh my!" She lifts out the silver charm bracelet with five little charms—two girls, three boys—each with a different color gem. "It's my children," she says, getting all teary eyed. "Oh, it's lovely." She looks on the tag that says *House of Lords*, then looks at Daddy, like maybe she thought he bought it for her. He just shrugs.

"And Daddy, this is for you." I hand him his own small box. He finds a silver belt buckle with the Blarney Castle engraved into the silver on the face of the buckle.

"Wow! This is incredible." He looks at Mama like maybe she bought it for him, but she just shrugs.

"Adriana." I hand her a small box as well. She lifts the lid and finds a glittery emerald green ring. I saw her eyeballing it the other day and knew she liked it.

"Oh, wow! Who knew I liked this?"

"Maybe Hans?" I said, just to throw her.

"Yeah," Benji chimes in, "Maybe it's a *ingagemint*

ring!"

Everyone laughs except Adriana, who is gawking over her new ring. And Mama and Daddy are looking a little concerned.

JR grabs the box with his name on it and tears into it. "Cool! A Swiss Army knife. I was just looking at this yesterday!"

Next, I hand Dino and Benji the biggest box and tell them it has both of their names on it, so they have to share. They both rip open the wrapping and pull the bear out of the box. I made a paper Viking hat and secured the little sword in his hand. "It's a Viking bear," I tell them.

They start fighting over who gets to hold him on the airplane home.

Adriana gets up and goes to get something in her room. She returns and tosses me a bottle of Bonnie Bell face toner. "Here, AJ, since you're always sneaking into my *Bonnie Bell*—and filling the bottle with water every time you use it—you might as well have it. Merry Christmas."

"Wow, thanks!" *How did she know I was always sneaking into it?* Guess maybe I over-did it a little on the water.

I realize I'm the only one who hasn't opened anything. "Oh, wow, look, it's for me!" I grab my gift and rip it open, just like I really would if it were from someone else. "Oh, wow! This is ad-o-o-o-r-able! How did anyone know I love mice?"

"Maybe you just resemble them so much, they took a wild guess."

"I am not a rodent," I inform Adriana.

She raises her eyebrows like that's debatable.

I refuse to be insulted. *"Ta' lucha gleoite."*

"What is that supposed to mean?"

"Mice are cute."

While everyone is looking happy with their gifts,

Mama and Daddy are looking puzzled. Mama leans over to Daddy and quietly says, "I can't imagine who would buy such expensive gifts for all of us—or know exactly what everyone wanted."

"I'm telling you, Soph, it had to be Santa," Daddy says.

"If it were Santa, I would have gotten a new Thunderbird."

"Only if Santa got a better day job." Daddy laughs.

Well, kids," Mama says, "It has been a wonderful trip and Christmas, but it's time we all pack and get ready for our trip home. Let's get our bags down to the lobby and join the others for a final bon voyage."

*

We are all in the lobby, waiting, while our Blarney Bus driver, Rory, loads our gear and takes us all back to the airport in Dublin. I'm not looking forward to another grueling bus ride.

A desk clerk looks over, and I remember my tab. I quietly tell Kaylee that I have a room charge I need to settle before we go.

"Oh, that won't be necessary right now, AJ. I've informed all of the parents that since everything is billed to Sugar Shamrock's corporate account, they will bill any additional room charges to your home address in the States once they settle the balance and convert it into dollars."

"Oh. Okay." *Phew! I've got more time to earn a little more cash before the bill arrives, just in case I went a little over twenty-five bucks.*

*

After being up past midnight and then getting up before dawn, I spend the entire bus ride back to Dublin in dreamland, with visions of sugarplums dancing in my head.

Our entire tour group is on the same flight back to

America, so at least I don't have to say long, tearful goodbyes in Ireland, except to Paddy. I will never forget little Paddy.

*

As our plane flies over the Atlantic Ocean, I make sure I know where to find my life cushion and oxygen mask, just in case. Then I look around at everyone on my plane: Tina's Tappers, the Yodel family, my family. After spending so much time together, I feel like we are all *cara cléibh're*. Good friends.

I was worried most of the time that no one in my family was having much fun, and that they blamed me for winning them a dumb trip. But, as I watch Dino and Benji play warrior Vikings with their bear, I realize they never knew about the Danish Vikings and the O'Donnell Clan before.

JR and Noah have become good mates, and plan to swap baseball cards with each other by mail when they get back home.

Mama and Daddy are toasting each other with cute little airplane bottles of Irish whiskey. *"Slante!"*

And Adriana is thumbing through her *Seventeen Magazine,* not looking as miserable as she did on the way here.

"Hey, AJ," she says, flipping the pages.

"Yeah?"

"Ireland wasn't quite as lame as I thought it would be."

"Really?"

"Yeah."

Wow. That coming from Adriana is almost like her saying *thank you.* Maybe Netti is right.

I turn and look out the window at the silver-lined clouds against the pure blue sky. I think of St. Patrick, and Finn the Giant, and all the Irish people singing *Danny Boy* to us. I think of the dancing, the music, and the sad potato famine, and how when I see Irish people in America now, I will know they came to America for a better life, just like my Italian grandparents did. I think of Netti and her story, and hope so much that she is right. I think of the dark, starry night with Paddy, and the shepherds, and Baby Jesus, and how I felt heaven and earth all at the same time. And I look up toward the One who brought us all here, and whisper, *"Go raibh maith agat."*

Thank You.

~

Thirty days later….

As soon as I walk in the door from school, I can hear Mama raising her voice in the other room.

What did Adriana do now? I wonder.

Dumping my school books on the counter, I notice a letter from Sugar Shamrocks:

Dear Degulio Family,

It is with great pleasure that we present your family with this special box of Sugar Shamrocks.

Oh my gosh! My eyes dart around the room until they land on the dining room table. There we are—all over the front of the cereal box! It's us!

We won, we won, we won!

And Adriana is *not* in the mini-dress, thank goodness. They must have used the original contest photo instead of our presentation night photo.

I am jumping up and down, about to scream....when I see another page with a list of charges:

Blarney Beag Boutique, Ireland

Irish Bear with dress $10

Emerald princess ring $50

Porcelain mouse tea party $15

Silver belt buckle $25

Miniature silver sword $10

Silver charm bracelet $30

Engraved Swiss army knife $10

Total due: **$150 US Dollars**

My jaw is still dropping when Adriana bursts into the room. "You have *ruined* my life! How can I face anyone ever again, knowing the entire world has seen me in that *ridiculous* jumper?"

"Not *everyone*. Only people who eat Sugar Shamrocks…" I offer.

JR walks in the back door and drops his books on the table next to the cereal box. I watch him take it in. "No. *No way. Not* on the box…in a *skirt!*"

"No one will remember this five years from now…"

"Ange͛   ͞uliana Degulio, is that you in there?" Mama yͦ   ͞ room.

 ͞ that bill from

An Deireadh

The End

Danny Boy

By Frederic Weatherly

Oh Danny boy, the pipes, the pipes are calling
From glen to glen, and down the mountain side
The summer's gone, and all the flowers are dying
'Tis you, 'tis you must go and I must bide.

But come ye back when summer's in the meadow
Or when the valley's hushed and white with snow
'Tis I'll be here in sunshine or in shadow
Oh Danny boy, oh Danny boy, I love you so.

But when ye come, and all the flowers are dying
If I am dead, as dead I well may be
You'll come and find the place where I am lying
And kneel and say an "Ave" there for me.

And I shall hear, tho' soft you tread above me
And all my grave will warm and sweeter be
For you will bend and tell me that you love me
And I shall sleep in peace until you come to me.

If you enjoyed the Degulio family in *AJ's Ireland*, you might also enjoy this first chapter of

SAVING SAILOR

From the SAVING SAILOR trilogy

Published by David C Cook Publishers 2007

Available in all major bookstores and on Amazon and Kindle

Introduction

When I was growing up, I thought I came from the weirdest family on earth. Now, as I look back on my childhood, I know I did. When I compare my family in those days with families of today, I see just how weird we really were. For one thing, there were seven of us, almost unheard of nowadays. For another, I had only *one* set of parents, and they actually loved each other. A lot. Scary, isn't it? And here's the real clincher … I had a *great* childhood. The kind where your mom stayed home and baked cookies for you, and your family stayed in a summer cabin *all summer*, and swam and water-skied and had candy night every Friday night.

What can I say …?

Pretty much, just, *Thank God.*

Did I mention we weren't perfect? Well, we weren't. But perfect isn't what makes a great childhood. What makes a childhood great is being able to look back and remember the good over the bad, the laughter over the tears, and the love that covered a multitude of sins.

It's looking back to that one summer that stands out above the rest. You know … the one where you knew what really mattered in life: God, your dog, your hamster, and your family. Most definitely in that order.

Prologue

Many times there comes into our life a crosswind, a change in course that changes us forever. Oftentimes we don't know until years later just how much influence that event had on who we have become.

For some of us it comes at a very young age; for others, late in life. For me, it came in the summer of 1968, when I was ten years old. It swept over me like an east wind when I was heading south. I can only describe it as an epiphany, an awakening in my young soul that told me there was something more to life than what I could see with my eyes.

Along with that awakening came the people and relationships that would determine how much or how little I would settle for in life, how far I would seek to find Truth. And true love. And the revelation that life is a wonderful gift of grace.

I look back on that summer often, when life feels more complicated than it should. The memories are never far from my heart and mind. I have only to close my eyes to see the water ... cool, clear blue water. And when I breathe, I smell the sweet, warm, summer air of my childhood ...

Drifting

Indian Lake, Idaho
July 1968

I'm sittin' in a rowboat in the middle of Indian Lake with my dog, Sailor. He's a collie-shepherd mix with one brown eye, and one that looks like a marble. He's wearin' a bright orange life jacket, as any seaworthy dog should when playing shipmate. Sometimes we pretend we're on the high seas awaitin' capture from handsome rogue pirates. But today, we're just driftin'.

The oars lay on the floorboard of the wood dinghy; a slight breeze sweeps over us, rufflin' up Sailor's long fur. We're just soakin' up the sun, and floatin' by the island where our family spends our summers.

My mama is reclinin' on the dock in her new Hollywood sunglasses. She's got a paperback novel in one hand and a glass of iced tea in the other. My big sister, Adriana, is slathering on baby oil, singin' along to her transistor radio. My big brother, J. R., short for Sonny Jr., is gutting a fish over on the big rocks, while the younger twins, Benji and Dino, are still tryin' to catch their first fish of the day.

All of this is going on, while at the same time I'm in the middle of a conversation with God:

"... And so Lord, if we get to pick what age we'll be in heaven, I choose nine years old, because I am havin' the best year of my life. I know I say that every year, but this time I mean it. And next year, if I change my mind, don't believe me. I promise it will always be nine."

I have this feelin' deep down inside that I will never change my mind. I just don't see how it can get any better than driftin' with my dog on a sunny afternoon, goin' wherever the wind takes us ...

1

Indian Island

"A. J., you float your little fanny right back to this dock."

"Comin', Mama," I yell across the water. I think we have a family matter we're about to deal with here. Our family tends to have a lot of family matters. If you ask me, it comes from havin' too much family history. There are times I just want to say, "ix-nay on the istory-hay." Nix on the history.

For starters: we are a Roman Catholic Italian family, and none of us are allowed to forget that. Anyone who puts that identification in jeopardy is dealt with severely. I was nearly disowned for trying to change my name to Dorothy Jones at school.

To make matters worse, there are two rumors I've had to live with my entire life. One is false. The other true. Contrary to what my sister has told everyone since the day I was born, my parents did not win me in a Mississippi bingo hall when I was a baby. And yes, my real name is Angelina Juliana Degulio.

I am a living legacy of two grandmothers who insist on preserving our *rich Italian heritage*. My name was settled in a coin toss. The dispute was over whose name would be first. Grandma Angelina won, but was accused of cheatin' by Grandma Juliana. They fight about it to this day.

The name Angelina, I am often reminded, means "angel," and I am the lucky child who gets to bear it. So, whenever someone asks me my name, I say, "Just call me A. J."

I'm workin' my way back to the dock, paddlin' with my arms over the bow of the boat. Once I'm in drift mode I like to stay there. "Still comin', Mama …"

The one thing I've gotten away with up to this very moment has been my self-imposed Southern accent. My mama is just beside herself right now from hearin' me yell, "I'm floatin' down yonder, Mama." I'm the only one of her kids to call her Mama instead of Mom, or use words like *y'all,* and *yonder.* I don't do it to make her mad. I just picked it up from those old Western movies I watch. I'm still tryin' to figure out why they call them Westerns, when everybody's talkin' Southern.

I think Southern is a beautiful language. I'm almost fluent now, but I have to watch it around Mama. Tends to get on her nerves. The closer I get to the dock, the more sure I am that "down yonder" musta really hit a nerve. You always know when you've gone too far with Mama. You can see the blood rise in her face like a thermometer on a hot day. And it just keeps risin' 'til her true Italian temper kicks in. Like right now ...

"Angelina Juliana Degulio ..."

That's the next clue—she yells the whole embarrassing name.

"No full-blooded *Roman Catholic Italian* child raised in the Northwest can possibly have a Southern accent. You stop that Southern garble right now before I march you into the confessional at St. Peter's, where you can tell Father Sharpiro how you're dishonoring your family." That's my mama's way of sayin', if I want to stay out here on the water, I'd better zip it with the Southern lingo. If there's one thing I've learned about Mama, she plays life by her rules. You either follow them or you're out of the game.

Her name is Sophia, and she would like everyone to believe that she is *The* Sophia Loren from Hollywood. When she does herself all up, she comes pretty close. She has those same dark Italian eyes, and adds that little swoosh of eyeliner. She even makes a point of getting her hair styled exactly like the actress's.

Mama's favorite game is to fool people into thinkin' she is Miss Loren. She can only go so long before she decides she just has to play this game or she will go nuts. If there's one thing Mama cannot tolerate, it's boredism. We'll all be layin' around the dock readin' or fishin', when suddenly, out of the blue we'll hear, "Miss Loren is goin' to town ..." Then she hauls us all off the island to go to town with her. We usually go somewhere real crowded, like downtown Squawkomish.

First off, we hit the corner across from the local hangout, Big Daddy Burger. Mama puts on her dark sunglasses, dabs on her Poppy Pink lipstick, and hands me a notepad and pen. "A. J.," she'll say, "after I get over there by that crowd, you all come running up to me holding out that notepad, yelling, 'Sophia, Sophia, can we have your autograph?'"

Adriana is so embarrassed she pretends she doesn't know us, but my brothers love this as much as I do. And, boy, do people fall for it. The next thing you know, everyone is swarmin' around my mama. Folks are pullin' anything they can out of their purses and pockets, even old gum wrappers, to get that autograph. The best part is, Mama says it's not even a sin because when people ask for her autograph she only signs her first name. She also says, "It serves these people right for being so gullible as to think that the real Sophia Loren would be spendin' her time at Big Daddy Burger, in downtown Squawkomish."

After she's done gettin' everybody riled up, we all pile into our turquoise Thunderbird convertible and laugh all the way to The Spaghetti House. Everyone, that is, but Adriana. I guess you can't expect a sixteen-year-old Prom Queen to think that's funny.

I'm watchin' Adriana right now from my boat. I can't believe how much time she spends just tryin' to get tan. That is really all she does all day—just lays there on that dock, with her iodine-tinted baby oil. It really makes no sense to me. She was born with a tan, for Pete's sake. She is already so dark, if you put a red dot on her forehead people would think she's from India.

Sometimes when I look at her, I wish I had dark hair and eyes like she does. I'm the only blondie in the bunch. People talk about Adriana with words like *beautiful*, or *striking*. I only hear words like *cute*, or names like *Freckles* when people talk about me. I also have this gap between my two big front teeth that makes me look like the guy on the front of *Mad* magazine. Mama says, "Who wants a white picket fence for a smile anyway?" The only good thing I can say about it is, I can squirt water between my front teeth farther than anyone I know, which comes in handy when you're livin' on a lake all summer.

I float past the dock pretendin' to be a fountain statue, squirtin' a stream of water straight up in the air. That really grosses out Adriana, which makes it even more fun.

"Take your big fat beaver teeth and go build yourself a dam," she yells.

My sister loves to torment me about my bingo hall beginnings, and says that's why I look and talk different from the rest of the family. "What more could we expect out of a Mississippi bingo hall, than a sappy little towhead with a Southern drawl?" She also points out my taste in music: "While everyone else is groovin' to the Beatles, there you are wallowing in 'Moon River.'"

Sometimes, when I feel different from the rest of the family I think of "Wolf Boy." It's a story I read about this little boy who got lost in the woods and was adopted and raised by a pack of wolves. When his family found him again, he acted more like his wolf family than his real family. I may be different, but I don't think I'm *that* different. To tell the truth, I wouldn't want to be like Adriana anyway. I would rather be out here floatin' with my dog, not worryin' about what color I'm turnin'. I get tired of watchin' Miss Perfect on the dock. I toss a stick for Sailor, and he jumps right out of the boat and swims after it. Adriana gives me a look like I am just so immature to be playing fetch with "that big dumb dog."

"Hey, Adriana," I yell, "can't you think of anything better to do than waste your whole day layin' in one place for a stupid tan?" Then I remind her that true beauty is more than skin deep, and maybe she should spend more time workin' on the inside.

She just yawns like it is hardly worth her time to respond, then says, "Oh, A. J., why don't you go join a convent or something?"

I smile when Sailor gets out of the water and shakes all over her. Wouldn't surprise me if they could hear her screamin' clear on the mainland. I load Sailor back into the boat. "Good dog," I whisper.

It doesn't bother me what Adriana thinks of my music, or anything else I happen to like. I am what Daddy calls "a hopeful romantic." I watch all those Westerns with The Duke, and just melt over the steamy love scenes where he's kissin' his girl.

Daddy tells me not to settle for anything less in a man than what I see right there on that TV screen. "You get yourself a man's man, A. J. There's a world full of wimps out there who will put on a pair of cowboy boots and call themselves a cowboy. You just make sure you find the one who can actually ride a horse."

I have never told anyone this, but, I have got the biggest crush on Little Joe Cartwright, from *Bonanza*. I love to daydream about him. That's one of my favorite things to do when I'm out here in my boat. I just close my eyes while I'm driftin' along, and the next thing I know … I'm his girl. He's comin' in from a long day of wrestlin' cows out on the Ponderosa, and I'm cookin' up some dead deer stew for him. He comes into my big ranch kitchen and says, "Boy, that sure smells good," with that romantic Southern accent of his. Then he comes over and gives me this big ol' kiss. We kiss so long, the stew just burns away on the stove, and we have to have peanut butter sandwiches instead.

Now, he may not be as big and burly as The Duke, but he is cute, cute, cute. That goes a long way in my book. Besides that, he can ride a horse.

Right in the middle of my daydream, I hear the sound of our boat engine and open my eyes. My daddy must have gotten off work early today, because he's pullin' up to the dock, and

it's not even four o'clock yet.

"Everybody in," he yells. "We're going for a ride."

I hear Adriana moan. She does not enjoy these family outings one bit. But Daddy had a talk with her last night about how we are a family, and like it or not, she needs to try and be a part of it. Then he told her how one day she will look back and miss these days, to which she rolled her eyes.

My daddy's name is Sonny. He's the park ranger at Indian Lake State Park on the main shore. We get to stay out here from the time school lets out in June, 'til it starts up again in September.

Daddy likes to call me Ficuccia. He was fed up with all the rivalry caused in choosin' my name, so he just came up with a name of his own. *Ficuccio* means "little fig" in Italian. Ficuccia would be a little girl fig, which is much easier to live up to than "angel."

Daddy's a big man with thick black wavy hair and deep blue eyes. When he's pullin' away from the dock, a ray of sunlight hits his eyes. They look just like two blue jewels shinin' back at me. "Daddy, what did the girls think of you when you were young?" I ask him.

He glances over at Mama, then says, "I was a knockout in high school. Your mother had to fight all the girls off of me just to get me to notice her." Daddy gives Mama a big grin and starts to laugh.

"Sonny Degulio, that's a bunch of hogwash and you know it. There were so many boys swarming around me, I couldn't see through 'em all to have even noticed you were alive." Then she added, "You wouldn't have had a chance if my mother hadn't forced me to marry you. You were her only ticket to Roman Catholic Italian grandbabies."

Daddy smiles at Mama. "Admit it, baby. I was hot. The Italian

Stallion, remember?"

Mama just rolls her eyes, but she's smilin' too. I think Daddy won Mama because he can make her laugh. Nobody can make Mama laugh the way Daddy can.

A lot of folks out here own their own cabins and boats, but we are renters all the way. My daddy says, "Why would I want to buy a boat when I can rent the African Queen every summer?"

When a boatful of girls go by, J. R. yells, "Duck down," to my little brothers. "We look like a boatful of sissies."

We are the only family I know on this lake with a pink boat. But Daddy says this was just like the boat they used in a famous movie, *The African Queen*, and we should sit up tall and proud when we pass other boats. "They only laugh because they're jealous."

So Mama says, "Well, Sonny, since you're feeling so high and mighty in your pink boat today, let's see how tall and proud you look when this big fancy yacht up ahead passes by."

Daddy looks at Mama real sly, then grabs his ranger hat. He jumps on the bow of the boat and pulls his ranger pants up to nearly his chest. Now his ankles are stickin' out with his bright green socks. He's just standin' out there with his face to the wind in his ranger hat, lookin' ridiculous. He's stickin' out his chest and holdin' his pants up by his thumbs, just waitin' for that yacht to pass by us. We are all howlin' so bad, we can't even hide our heads.

So here comes the yacht right close to our boat, and people are lookin' at us like we are from *Mars*, and Daddy yells, "'Afternoon, gentlemen. I know what y'all are thinkin', but there is no way we will trade our African Queen for your yacht, so don't even think about it."

Now Mama's laughin' so hard she just rolls right off her boat cushion onto the floor. That just makes us laugh harder. But Mama can't stop, and she sure as anything can't get up off the floor. So Daddy hops down off the bow to help her up, but she can't even take his hand. Then Daddy asks, "What's so funny, darlin'?" with an accent just like mine.

Mama can hardly talk, but she squeaks out, "Do you know who that was?"

Daddy says, "No Soph, I don't. Why don't you tell me?"

So, Mama squeals, "Dr. Starky ..." and she's laughin' so hard now she's cryin'.

The reason that might seem so funny to Mama is because Dr. Starky already thinks we're a pretty nutty family, even before Daddy yelled from the bow in his high-waters. See, we've only been here for one month, and we've been to Dr. Starky's three times. The first time was when Benji got a fishin' hook caught in his bare back when Dino was casting. He was screamin' like a banshee. We couldn't pull it out without tearin' up his back, so we just cut the line, and walked him into Dr. Starky's office with a fishhook stickin' outta his back.

Then on the Fourth of July, J. R. shot off a bottle rocket that went haywire and singed off part of his eyebrow. He was lucky he didn't lose his eye, but that put the kibosh on our Fourth of July. So once more we visited Dr. Starky with a weird injury.

Then, just last week, Dino had the great idea of pretendin' the island was his own private jungle, and Benji was the intruder who needed to be trapped and tortured. Once Benji stepped into his lasso, Dino pulled it tight around his ankle, and dragged his captured prey back to base camp for Chinese water torture. Unfortunately, along the way, he was dragged through a beehive, at which point Dino dropped the rope and ran for it, leavin' Benji to fend for himself. Benji came screamin' through the woods, followed by a swarm of bees, and his rope in tow. By the time he reached the cabin, he had so many bee stings Mama just threw him in the tub and soaked him in baking soda and meat tenderizer. A few hours later his whole face started to swell. When he walked into Dr. Starky's office, Benji looked like somethin' from *My Favorite Martian*. By the time Mama stopped laughin' at him, Dr. Starky was lookin' at her like she was just the worst mother in the whole world to laugh at her son like that.

What Dr. Starky doesn't understand about our mama is, when she starts to laugh about somethin' you really aren't supposed to laugh about, tryin' to stop only makes it worse. She said she's been that way since she was a kid, and has gotten in a lot of trouble for laughin' in school, church and libraries, even at funerals. Daddy's gotten pretty good about walkin' her out of those situations once it starts, because when she gets to laughin' like that, she's too weak to get up and run out herself.

After Mama recovers from seeing Dr. Starky on the yacht, she says, "Well, Sonny, if that man didn't already have enough doubts about this family, you just clinched the deal for us." She tells Daddy that the best part is yet to come because Daddy has to go to his office to get his mandatory tetanus shot for work next week.

Daddy says, "Well, maybe I'll just wear my Smokey Bear outfit for the occasion."

For *Saving Sailor*

and sequels;

Taking Tuscany

Heading Home

Visit

<u>Books by Renee Riva</u>

If you would like to receive new release notices email
reneeriva@gmail.com